A S

The nettles were as tall as Peter. A disproportionate feeling of hugeness began to trouble him, as if he had shrunk, or the countryside expanded. Suppose some great beast was to come out of the trees at him, some really gigantic stag or buffalo or mammoth and he should reach no higher than its knee?

He began to sweat as he told himself not to be absurd. But there was something wrong: *This is a bad place*. He nearly said it out loud: he felt it now in his guts, in his bones.

Also by Nina Beachcroft

Under the Enchanter
A Visit to Folly Castle
Well Met by Witchlight

Nina Beachcroft

A SPELL OF SLEEP

> *Very old are we men;*
>   *Our dreams are tales*
> *Told in dim Eden*
>   *By Eve's nightingales;*
> *We wake and whisper awhile,*
>   *But, the day gone by,*
> *Silence and sleep like fields*
>   *Of amaranth lie.*

WALTER DE LA MARE

MAMMOTH

First published in Great Britain 1976
by William Heinemann Ltd
Published 1991 by Mammoth
an imprint of Mandarin Paperbacks
Michelin House, 81 Fulham Road, London SW3 6RB

Mandarin is an imprint of Reed International Books Ltd

Copyright © Nina Beachcroft 1976

The author and publishers wish to thank the Literary
Trustees of Walter de la Mare, and The Society of
Authors as their representative, for permission to
quote from 'All That's Past' by Walter de la Mare.

ISBN 0 7497 0714 3

A CIP catalogue record for this title
is available from the British Library

Printed in Great Britain
by Cox & Wyman Ltd, Reading, Berkshire

1

'Aren't you coming, then?'

'No.'

'Oh, please yourself.'

The other boys went off across the green, passing the football to one another, leaving Peter idly kicking a stone on the footpath. He had not wanted to go with them because he was brooding over his wrongs and had not felt like being one of a noisy group, but now, despite himself, he was just a little annoyed that they could get on without him so easily.

Hating everybody and everything, even the weather, because it was sunny and cheerful and refused to fit in with his mood, Peter turned round and began to walk away from the village down the bridleway between the double hedges. He was not going to return for some time, if ever. His mother and beastly sisters could just lump it. Why should his mother take Janice and Linda's side against him? Always, always this was so. It had been an entire accident anyway, his breakage of the dolls' teacups. Somebody should have understood this. But he was not going to tell them now how they had misjudged him.

Peter found a stick and began to slash at brambles and nettles as he went. There was a big prickly teasel growing by the path. He had it down in an instant. He brought some big heads of cow parsley toppling to the ground in ruin, which was satisfactory. Then he went on, following the bridleway which meandered between fields of barley, wheat and occasionally cows. After a time he came to the blackberry bushes he and his sisters picked at the end of every summer: the fruit was only just forming now. He slashed around for a few minutes at the bottom of the brambles and then walked on again.

The bridleway crossed a lane and continued by the side of a field of barley. Peter crossed the lane too, hesitated a moment and then followed it. He had now passed beyond where he had previously walked on foot. His family were not great walkers. Of course he had been driven about the countryside time and again and he had bicycled down nearly every road and lane for miles – but actually walking, and alone at that, it just so happened he had not gone in for it much.

So very soon the countryside began to take on an unfamiliar look, although of course he knew the general direction in which he must be heading. The land was a little deceptive here; gently rolling, it displayed before him more slopes and valleys and patches of woodland than he had thought to exist.

'I don't care!' said Peter to himself, slashing at some tall nettles that barred the way. He sneezed as the piercing scents of summer, of grass and nettles, dog roses and poppies, penetrated his nose. 'Atishoo! So what, if nobody likes me or wants me?' For it wasn't just his family who misunderstood him: his so-called friends had only the other day insulted him deeply by calling him a snob and a swot and a teacher's pet, and all because he liked to be on his own, and liked reading sometimes. Well, if he were different, he was proud of it, so there. It did not worry him, not likely. Nor did it worry him that he had not grown much of late, and that Janice, though a year and a half younger, was nearly as tall as he. He would start growing again some time. But when?

He knocked down the tallest tops of some grasses and willowherb growing at the verge of the path, bringing them down to size. The small plants underneath them he let alone.

The bridleway had dwindled to a path which led uphill to a small wood with a broad ditch running round it and a low bank above. It was a dark, silent wood without much undergrowth. At the centre of the wood Peter came to a clearing where someone must have been digging; soft, peaty earth was piled up on one side and there were a good many large flinty stones about. Funny to find great stones like these here in the middle of a wood. In one place they looked as if they had formed the beginning of a wall. It was all a bit of a mess. And so very quiet in here – apart from a constant humming, buzzing sound. The hum changed to a high-pitched whine as a mosquito dived suddenly at him and Peter decided that he didn't want to be stung to death. The path had stopped completely but he forced his way through clutching brambles out of the little wood to an empty meadow beyond. He was beginning to get a little tired and hungry but he was not going to turn back yet.

Thinking about it afterwards as he was to do so many times, he came to the conclusion that it was some time not so long after the mosquito-y wood that he began to become aware of a change.

To begin with it began to get unpleasantly warm. The wind dropped altogether and the sun muffled itself behind high white clouds and seemed to radiate the same stuffy heat equally from all parts of the sky. Silence can take a time to penetrate, then it gets thicker and thicker. He had walked through the wood which had been very quiet apart from the humming, but it seemed even quieter on emerging from the wood: no birds twittering or cawing, no beasts in the fields, no aeroplanes, not even a bee. A heavy, waiting silence. The path continued: trees and rough scrub on one side, a field with something growing in it on the other, and for the first time Peter thought of going back. But something kept him wandering slowly onwards. The field beside him had beans growing in it, but what a mess they were! No farmer could harvest this crop. Half of them were smashed and mangled into the ground, the rest black and mouldy. Storms within the last week had brought heavy rain and some destruction and this had dented and lowered some of the barley he had passed earlier in the morning, but nothing like this blackness and death . . . It *was* quiet.

'Half a league, half a league, half a league onward,' he began to chant to himself, perhaps to dispel the faint stirrings of unease that were beginning to bother him:

> 'Into the valley of death
>   Rode the six hundred.'

They did not question the orders, they did not care – how did it go? He had forgotten.

'*In*to the valley of death.'

He stopped singing out loud but other words went on in his mind:

> 'Brightness falls from the air
>   Queens have died young and fair
> . . . I am sick   I must die
>   Lord have mercy on me!'

He had read that somewhere: a long poem, in the school library perhaps. The trouble with the school library was that not all that many people wandered into it and so when one did, one was noticed. That silly Miss Everett coming up and speaking to him and asking him what books he liked when he just wanted to be left alone! It was enough to make one stop ever going in there again.

> 'Brightness falls from the air,
>   Queens have died young and fair.
> Dust hath closed Helen's eye,
>   I am sick   I must die
>   Lord have mercy on me!'

And then, as he was mumbling and muttering to himself, not quite liking for some reason to sing out loud and make a great noise, these words began to speak themselves in his brain:

> 'Ten long years of sleep
>   Bed them soft and deep
> Cover them with the sky
>   Drain their deadly malice dry.'

What was that? Where had he read that? What could it mean? And goodness, it was warm: the heat was making the air about him shimmer. Heat hazes were odd things. They were all about him wherever he looked, towering high above a patch of rank long grass and nettles. The nettles were as tall as Peter. A disproportionate feeling of hugeness began to trouble him, as if he had shrunk, or the countryside expanded. Suppose some great beast was to come out of the trees at him, some really gigantic stag or buffalo or mammoth and he should reach no higher than its knee?

He began to sweat as he told himself not to be absurd. But – there was something wrong: *This is a bad place.* He nearly said it out loud: he felt it now in his guts, in his bones. It was not his imagination. He was not imaginative. *He would not be imaginative.*

If only a wind would start up and move those motionless bunches of leaves, those reeds and grasses that looked as if they had been carven, ripple the dark greasy surface of that stagnant pool. Here was another field of something growing – or attempting to grow. Oats and grass mingled and again were trampled, sodden, tangled and useless. From the signs a herd of animals had wandered here unchecked – but where were they now?

And then there came a moment when Peter knew that he was very frightened indeed.

He should never have come here. Somehow or other he had got into a place of dreadful wrongness.

He must return, but by which path? He looked round in bewilderment. The forest – he thought of it now as a forest – had closed up around the strips of field: if he went to the right where there was another clearing of sorts and yes, a cottage, he could see the thatch, it might help him get his bearings. So Peter ran in something very nearly approaching panic, into the clearing.

The clearing was not very big and entirely surrounded by trees. A patch of high grass, bleached and brown as if it were dying, stretched for several yards before a very old and decrepit-looking cottage with a thatched roof and rough wood and plaster walls. It had only two windows and they were tiny, dark glassless holes. Against the cottage on one side was a pile of dusty straw, on another a kind of lean-to shed: the yard just before the cottage was of trampled earth and straw, but as he approached through the waist-high grass it was not at the cottage that Peter looked, because through the grass stems he had caught sight of what looked like a foot, bare and filthy: he walked nearer, despite the shock it gave him, and now he had come upon the body. Lying in front of the cottage was a fat man clothed in rough, odd clothes, the details of which Peter did not take in because his heart was pounding so with shock. But the man was not dead as Peter had at first thought and which he could not have borne.

He was fast asleep: the mound of his fat stomach rising and falling. He was snoring gently, his mouth open, showing broken and discoloured teeth. He was not a young man: the stubble of his beard was greyish. And then near the open dark cavern of the door, Peter saw an over-turned wooden tub and sprawled beside it, a woman also fast asleep. She lay on her front, hunched in what looked an uncomfortable position, her long skirts rumpled and showing one bare and hairy fat leg. She had rough wooden clogs upon her feet.

They were a dirty, strange-looking couple. Peter stared at them for a few minutes: he did not like the look of them. He became aware of a very strong disinclination to wake them up or have anything to do with them. Nor did he want to turn his back on them and leave them lying here like this. So cautiously he came nearer still, into the yard.

Now he was standing very near the sleeping man, watching with a kind of fascinated repulsion the breath whistling in and out through his half-open mouth. He looked a little like an elderly pig; his nose and mouth went together into a kind of snout. He had a wart on his forehead. His dirty, greyish hair receded, his –

A movement behind him, or what Peter fancied was a movement behind him, something at any rate that made his stomach lurch suddenly in fright caused him to start forward, to stumble, to fall indeed right over the sleeping man's stomach. He was up again in an instant, but the damage had been done. There was nothing behind him but the man grunted, stirred, and then suddenly sat up.

'Wha– wha– do yer,' he growled indistinctly and his hand abruptly shot out and caught Peter's leg.

'Hey, no, let me go!' Peter shouted in fright, and kicked himself loose.

The man was rising to his feet, yawning and looking bewildered. 'Eh, but what's amiss? Where's the old bitch?–' He strode to his wife and kicked her until she moved. He screwed his hands into his eyes and looked up at the sky and then at Peter. 'I know you, or I think I do: you're like enough,' he remarked and sent an unpleasant chill up Peter's spine. 'What 'ave you done? It's late by the sky. 'Ere, arouse yourself, woman.' And he proceeded to haul his wife to her feet where she too stood scratching her head and yawning.

Up till now Peter had not seen her face distinctly, but now he did and there was something about its fat, bloated creases and the little dark eyes and the pouting lips beginning to stretch into a smile which upset and frightened him even more than the man had done. And then the whole horror of the past half-hour and the awakening of this dreadful couple overcame him so that he cried out and ran and ran without looking back, without looking anywhere much, and he banged into trees and splashed through puddles and fell into bushes and on and on, his heart pounding and bells ringing in his ears, while in his mind a coarse voice with a strange, thick accent kept saying, 'I know you, or I think I do. I know you . . .'

2

'Keep the curtains drawn if the light bothers your eyes and stay in bed until tomorrow morning, and by then I should hope that you'll be feeling a good deal better,' said the doctor briskly, closing his bag. 'It's only a very mild concussion. You must look where you're going next time, mustn't you?'

Peter smiled weakly, feeling a fool. He had arrived home two hours ago, with bruises on him which he could not account for and a lump upon his head which had probably been caused by his running full tilt into a tree. He could not exactly remember what had happened since he had run in panic from the clearing where he had awoken the sinister-seeming elderly couple. Somehow he had stumbled on and arrived home; it had taken a long time and he was not quite sure how he had managed it. The aspirins he had taken for the pain in his head were beginning to make him pleasantly sleepy and he did not want to think about anything much. He could just hear his mother's receding voice as she followed the doctor downstairs.

'Silly thing of him to do, wasn't it? I must admit he gave me a fright when he came in because he seemed so confused as to what had happened, and he was dreadfully late for dinner too, but I suppose he must have fallen out of a tree or something like that. Boys! You never know what they'll be up to next, do you?'

There was a blur of voices as the doctor answered and then the sound of the front door shutting. Peter's bedroom door opened and his ten-year-old sister put her head in:

'Whatever happened to you then?' she inquired curiously.

'Nothing. Shut up.'

'Needn't be so bad tempered. Shut up yourself, then.'

'Well, go out, get on – '

'Did you really climb up a tree?'

'Get *OUT*.'

'I don't want to, so there.'

At her most irritating, she tossed her long hair back but showed no sign of moving.

'I shall stay here as long as I like. You've no right to shout at me like that.'

But then their mother came up the stairs saying crossly:

'Janice, leave Peter alone, do you hear me?' and Peter who had turned his face to the wall heard heavy breathing for a few seconds as she sought to delay obeying her mother's command, then the door slammed with a noise that didn't hurt his head as much as it would have earlier and he drifted off to sleep.

When he awoke it was much later and he could hear the subdued rumble of voices coming from the kitchen which was immediately below his little back bedroom. It was six o'clock and they must be having their evening meal. This made him feel hungry and a little neglected and lonely. He had better go down and have something too. But before going down, he looked out of the window, down the garden towards the orchard. The sky was dark grey and mournful and the branches of the trees were agitated this way and that by the wind. Most of the trees were old and had already lost parts of themselves: winds like these were dangerous at this time of year when the weight of fruit and leaves could snap off an arm or a hand with all its trailing draperies. Why had he thought of it like that? Trees were just trees after all. They did not feel.

'Hey!' shouted Peter opening the door abruptly, and calling loudly down the stairs because he wanted to make a cheerful noise, because he didn't want to be alone any more. 'Don't I get anything to eat then? Are you going to let me starve to death or something?'

The next morning was Sunday; he felt all right and got up as usual and they had relatives visiting for the day, so it went in a whirl. The next day was Monday and school again and he was obviously perfectly well, so he went to school just like any other Monday.

By then his strange experiences on Saturday had receded into the background, pushed there by the ordinariness of a commonplace school morning. He had completely accepted everybody else's version of the accident.

He had a very ordinary Monday at school, made more unpleasant than sometimes by his omission of his maths homework over the weekend: if he had been too ill to do it he should have had a note from his mother to that effect: blah blah, Mr Somerville was a naggy old man. Peter brooded over this injustice in the coach on the way home, not joining as he sometimes did in the changeover of places and general mucking about when the large contingent got off at Pipers End, leaving just the few Long Green boys and girls behind them.

The last mile to Long Green was always a pleasant one. There was a satisfactory feeling of homecoming. The coach had left the main road and was climbing up and up between large fields of barley. The wind was rippling the barley in little thrills and tremors so that it looked almost as if some great beast were twitching its muscles and shaking its pelt. The backbone of the beast could be at the ridge of the hill over there . . . If one went over that hill, down the other side, up another slope and kept going for another mile or so, one might be somewhere not so very far from that walk. Little patches of sunlight were racing over the barley, changing its colour. He had now the oddest kind of feeling about his walk: as if there were more to remember about that strangely neglected tract of countryside he had wandered into: it must be *somewhere* over there, but would he ever find it again? It was as if the sunlight and shadow were running fitfully over his brain, lighting up some parts of it, leaving the rest misty and dull.

Important, interior things can happen very quickly. It was only another couple of minutes up into the village but by the

14

time the coach had come to a juddering stop and a last great pant of breath in its usual place near the post office and village shop, Peter knew at last and without any possibility of doubt that something that would forever alter him and the way he saw things had taken place on Saturday: he was not now quite the same boy who had gone out early in the day and had quarrelled with his sisters. That whole squabble was trivial, unimportant, compared to what had happened afterwards.

Mechanically he got up and followed the six boys and eight girls who made up the secondary school contingent from his village and who were now filing along the long body of the coach.

As he got down slowly and last of all, he saw his two sisters coming out of the shop, each clutching an ice lolly. The primary school in the village had ended half an hour ago.

'Peter, Peter, we've got something to tell you.' It was the seven-year-old, Linda, who came up to him first, while Janice, with whom he so often quarrelled, hung back, bit off the top of her lolly and said acidly: 'Oh, he'll find it out for himself soon enough.'

'Why, what's happened?'

'We didn't know anything about it till we came back for lunch and there was a car there, and now there's a van and now they're moving in!'

'*Who* are moving in, for heaven's sake – '

The girls had approached to walk on each side of him and talk across him.

'The new *people* of course,' said Linda impatiently.

'The new people next door to *us* she means,' put in Janice in a superior way. 'Not just new people in the village. New people in the house next to us. In Peacehaven. Mrs Joyce's Peacehaven, of course.'

'Oh no!' Peter's heart sank and he was jerked instantly back into the everyday world. 'Oh what a drag. Now we can't go over the garden and pick the raspberries.'

'Now we can't get our balls back easily,' chimed in Janice.

'*Now* Taptoes will be turned away from all her mouse holes,' added Linda sadly, for whom the family cat was an especial pet. 'They might not like her sitting on their flowerbeds.'

It certainly appeared to be a piece of bad news.

'I hadn't heard anything about anybody moving in,' said Peter with a feeling of injustice, as if he should have been warned. 'Did Mum know anything about it? She didn't tell *me*.'

'She said it took her quite by surprise,' cried Janice. 'She said she knew Mrs Joyce's daughter was going to let it again some time, but she thought there was going to be more work done on the outside first.'

'Oh,' said Peter, digesting this. 'Well, I think they ought to have *had* work done on the outside first. A lot of work. It needs it all right.'

Preferably work that would have taken all summer: that would have ensured the continued emptiness of Peacehaven: this was what lay behind Peter's words.

'And there aren't going to be any children,' put in Linda sadly. 'Just some old couple or other.'

'They might have been dreadful children anyway,' snapped Janice. 'I *personally* wouldn't have wanted anything to do with them.'

They had now reached the other end of the long village street and turned up a rough unmade-up road with fields on one side and three bungalows on the other: first the Browns' bungalow, in front of which the two Brown children were tricycling, then Oakdene, with its big oak tree, which was used now only for weekends, and lastly Mr North's bungalow, its garden as usual spotless and fruitful to the last centimetre. Mr North's back was bent double over his rose bushes. However, he straightened and gave them a smile as they passed. He was a nice old man. Then there was a small strip of orchard with a friendly white nannygoat in it which also belonged to Mr North, who had occasionally given their

16

mother cheese made from the goat's milk. Sometimes they passed the time of day with this goat, but today she was on the other side of her domain, under the trees. The road curved round and so they came upon their own house, beyond which was nothing more than the farm and its outbuildings and fields.

Their own house was large, Victorian and semi-detached: each part of it set in ample strips of garden with room at the bottom for the orchard of aged plum and apple trees which must have all been planted at the same time and made the two gardens look as if they were one. First they passed the half of the house that was called Peacehaven, with its own little white gate, long front path, two steps to the front door and the big bay window of its sitting room and front bedroom, and then beyond it, and identical, their own house Nut End, so named because of the old walnut tree in its front garden, by the privet hedge. People laughed at you for living at Nut End and called it 'Nutty End' and 'the Nut House' and all sorts of silly things like that to prove how funny they were, but Peter liked the name. He was fond of his house: he had been born there and it was impossible to imagine living anywhere else. Three years ago it had been very exciting because his parents had saved up enough money to buy Nut End from old Mrs Joyce who had owned both houses and lived herself in Peacehaven. Buying Nut End instead of renting it had not actually made much difference except that Peter's father had been very busy inside for a time improving the kitchen and scullery.

And then in February old Mrs Joyce had died, and so Peacehaven had become empty and they had grown accustomed to its emptiness. As spring advanced, the greenness and lushness of its growth had hidden their cautious forays through the gaps in the hedge into Peacehaven's garden. The gooseberries had dropped unpicked from the bushes, and at last they had had permission from Mrs Joyce's daughter who had inherited the house but lived in London to make what use of them they wished. And so gradually they had all come to

17

think of Peacehaven's garden almost as their own, except that nobody did the lawn and it had turned into a wild tangle of grass and dock, and nettles had grown all along under the old bit of washing line and by the dustbin.

So Peacehaven was occupied again. As Peter drew near his pace slowed and he gave it as long a stare as he could manage without actually stopping outside its front gate.

'Look, there's one of them looking out,' said Linda.

'Don't stare!' hissed the self-conscious Janice.

Peter caught a glimpse of a whitish blob of a face looking out from behind a dark red curtain which had already been put up and drawn nearly halfway across Peacehaven's big front window.

'It looks different already,' he said. 'Horrible. They've spoilt it.'

Otherwise there was no other sign that Peacehaven had been moved into. The removal van had gone and there were no other curtains up as yet. The garage door was shut.

'Yes, they've got a car, an old one,' said Janice, seeing his glance towards the garage. 'They drove it in.'

'There's my mum,' cried Linda, running down the garden path of Nut End. 'Where are you going to? Come back inside and give me my tea.'

'Just a moment,' said their mother, smiling and gently pushing away her youngest child. 'I was just popping round next door to introduce myself and ask if they'd like a cup of tea. I don't know if they've got the electricity on in there yet. The place must be awfully dusty to move into as nobody seemed to come in first and clean it up. I hope they'll settle in all right.'

'I'm going in,' announced Linda, and disappeared while Peter and Janice stood and watched their mother walk, a little more formally and stiffly than usual as if she knew she were being watched by other eyes as well as theirs, up the brick path of their garden, through the gate, then back through the gate of Peacehaven and down their path until she had reached the two steps up to the front door. It would have been much simpler of course to have stepped straight over a flower bed and over the three-foot fence that segregated the two gardens in front, but this she obviously could not do. She rang the bell of Peacehaven. There was a pause, and then suddenly the door opened and a voice said rather gruffly, 'Well?'

'May I introduce myself?' Peter and Janice heard their mother say, rather over-brightly, and they realized she was a little shy. 'I'm your next-door neighbour, Jean Turner. I wondered if I could make you a cup of tea or do anything to help?'

There was a silence, during which Janice and Peter heard their mother clear her throat nervously. They could see nothing of whoever was behind the door of Peacehaven, but heard a muffled call from somewhere within the house.

'Who is it? What's she want?'

'She wants to give us a cup of tea.'

'Oh – ' Something else; inaudible.

The door of Peacehaven opened wider and a figure came out on to the steps.

'Thank you very much I'm sure but we are perfectly well provided for.'

The speaker was a man in late middle age in grey flannel trousers, a shirt and maroon-coloured cardigan with carpet slippers upon his feet. He had a small bristly grey moustache and bushy grey eyebrows from beneath which his little eyes looked first at Peter's mother and then around and about until they fell on Peter. Peter's mouth was open and he stared and stared; all considerations of politeness forgotten. Because the man's face had given him a totally unexpected shock. It *was* – no, but of course not, it couldn't be. There was only a resemblance: catching him unawares just for the moment. How could he ever confuse two such different people: one the apparition of a dream, a concussion-nightmare of some kind, the other a perfectly normal respectable middle-aged man? And now he had put his foot in it by staring so rudely because the man looked at him a moment longer, gave a little laugh and said in no very agreeable voice, 'Well, you'll know me again, won't you, Sunny Jim,' and without another word he then went inside his door and shut it.

Peter's mother, looking rather pink, came back by the two paths, and when she got to Peter and Janice, she said '*Well*,' half to them and half to herself and then she said crossly to Peter, 'For goodness sake Peter didn't you ever know it wasn't manners to stare at people,' and to Janice she said, 'Oh come Janice get inside for goodness sake do and let's all have our teas,' and so they went inside and all of them tried to pretend in their different ways that nothing much had happened and in the end it was Linda, who had been in the house all the time, who said it: 'I don't think our new neighbours are very nice at all.'

'I don't exactly fancy him,' replied her mother, frowning slightly, 'but perhaps the woman is more friendly. I might catch her out in the garden and have a chat, or something. But if they want to keep themselves to themselves, well, let them, that's what I say.'

But they did not see the woman for a week, except as a face peering occasionally from the front window or a shape behind the bedroom net curtains staring down the back garden. The windows of Peacehaven overlooked nearly all Nut End's garden, except one strip at the far side. This had not seemed to matter when Mrs Joyce had the house; now it did.

One afternoon Linda came running in from the garden.

'I was on the swing,' she said, 'and that Mrs What's-'er-name . . .'

'Mrs Baxter,' supplied the alert Janice. 'Yes, what, Linda? Mrs Baxter what?'

'Mrs Baxter was looking out the window and she made a face at me.'

'Don't be so silly, Linda,' scolded Janice. 'Mrs Baxter wouldn't do a thing like that, she's a grown-up.'

'She did, she did, and I didn't like it and so I've come in.'

'Nonsense,' said Janice firmly, but she went out into the garden to see what she could see, rather excited, and privately resolved to make a face back at Mrs Baxter should one be needed.

'She's not there now,' she cried, coming in again very soon with a disappointed expression. 'She's not looking at us at all, so you can go out again, Linda.'

'I don't want to, anyway,' said Linda and she stayed indoors the rest of the afternoon.

It was Peter who first saw Mrs Baxter outside her house.

He had his bicycle upended in a cosy patch of sunlight between two bushes, and was trying to locate a puncture in its back tyre. Separating the houses at the back was a hedge, about five feet in height, thick in some places and thin almost to the point of non-existence in others.

Peter chanced to look up and a part of what he had taken to be the hedge on the Peacehaven side of him moved. It was a thinnish place in the hedge and she was standing to one side of the thin patch, looking into the garden of Nut End. The moment she saw Peter had noticed her, she moved, ducking her head slightly and giving him what he described afterwards to Janice as 'a rather loony smile'. For to tell the truth she and her smile and her white face had startled him. But it was silly to be frightened by a dowdy, rather heavy, middle-aged woman, the kind you simply did not notice if you passed her in the street.

Janice took him up eagerly on the 'loony smile'.

'I think she's batty,' she said. '*Personally*. She's always staring at something in our garden. Or us. Like a cow. You can see her jaws moving, as if she were chewing the cud. And then she smiles. Like this.'

And Janice's sharp, bright little face was pulled askew in a passable imitation of Mrs Baxter's smile.

'Don't!' shouted Peter to her suddenly.

'Why not?' she shouted back shrilly. 'What did I do wrong now?'

21

'I'm *sorry* – ' Now he had got her all cross and resentful: it didn't take much. 'I didn't mean – it's just that, you gave me a start, copying her like that.'

'Oh,' said Janice dubiously, wriggling her shoulders, not sure how to react. 'Well, that's how she *was*.'

'Oh forget it,' muttered Peter, pushing past her and going into his room and shutting the door. He had to be alone. He had said 'a start' but it had been more like a shiver, a cold hand down his back. He did not know why the imitation of a rather meaningless smile should be so upsetting and indeed frightening: what indeed was there about one dumb-looking woman in late middle age, although she had a white toad-like face, to inspire anybody with such unease? And yet she had something about her to make the flesh creep: even the obvious aggression and unpleasantness of her husband seemed more acceptable, more *natural* than she.

3

Outside the rain pelted down, the windows streamed with it, the clouds were low and dark grey. Inside there were far too many people, thought Peter gloomily. He wished they didn't have to have relations in for the day on Sunday. Today there was Uncle Ron and Aunty Sheila and their two children, one a squalling babe in arms brought to be cooed and exclaimed over, the other an objectionable boy of five. His name was Justin. Although he was a cousin, Peter, Janice and Linda all united in detesting him.

'It *is* a pity about the rain,' said Mrs Turner for the third or fourth time. 'I'd hoped the children could be all out in the garden. Now, Sheila, I hope you'll take a glass of sherry? And, Ron, I think Jim has some beer, if you'd prefer that.'

'I'll have a gin and tonic, Jean, if it's all the same,' said Aunty Sheila, pirouetting on her high heel and smoothing her bright pink dress over her swelling hips. 'Ow, Justin, don't *do* that.' Her son was butting her in the stomach with his head. His face emerged for a moment to say crossly, 'Nothing to *do* , nothing to *do* here.'

'I'm so sorry, Sheila,' said Mrs Turner, looking harassed. 'I'm afraid we've only the sherry. We don't generally keep much of a stock in the house as I don't drink at all.'

'The sherry then, Jean, that will be fine.' Aunty Sheila's beautifully manicured hands with their several rings and charm bracelets and bright pink nails pushed ineffectually at her son.

'Justin, leave Mother alone,' said her husband, Uncle Ron, beer mug in his hand. He was younger brother to Mr Turner; the two men, stocky and dark, looked alike except that Jim Turner was now greying and looked tireder and less plump and sleek than his brother. Peter quite liked his Uncle Ron, he was hearty, good-natured, and always tried to keep the peace if there was any family squabble or disagreement. If they could just have Uncle Ron on his own without wife and family Peter would not have minded.

Lunch itself was not too bad except that Justin would not eat anything upon his plate and there was too much fuss made about it: both from people trying to tempt him and then from Aunty Sheila talking at length about all the things he would and would not eat, as if anyone cared. Then to make up for not having had his first course he was given three helpings of pudding: thus leaving no second helping at all for Peter and Janice who looked at each other in deeply sympathetic aggrievement but who did not like to complain. They had never been allowed to be one tenth as rude as Justin automatically was to everyone: it simply was not fair.

When he had golloped his pudding Justin got up from the table and began to run round it, pretending he was an aeroplane, making zooming noises and with his arms outstretched.

'Perhaps you'd like to go and do that in the sitting room, Justin, there doesn't seem much room for flying in here,' suggested his father mildly.

'Don't like their sitting room much, can we go home now?'

'No, of course we can't, Justin,' said his mother. 'Look, can't you come and sit down again like a good boy?'

Justin looked at her coolly for a moment, made a rude noise with his lips and to everyone's relief ran out of the room.

'You see, he doesn't like to get bored for a moment, his brain is so active,' explained Aunty Sheila. She went over to the carrycot in which her baby daughter had started to whimper, and picked her up.

'If I could just have her bottle warmed, Jean,' she said, holding the baby on her knee and continuing to talk about Justin. 'It's the penalty he pays for being so exceptionally clever: his teacher thinks his IQ to be quite 140. And of course we don't want to cross him too much and stifle his brain and his talents just as they're developing, because they say you mustn't do that, don't they?'

A silence greeted this remark: then Mrs Turner returned from the kitchen with the warm bottle.

'Wouldn't you be more comfortable feeding her on the sofa in the sitting room?' she suggested. 'And I'll bring us all coffee in there. No, don't bother to clear anything away. The children will help me later on.'

'You are silly, Mummy,' hissed Linda privately to her mother as they all got up and prepared to go into the next room. 'Justin's in there. If we'd stayed in the dining room we'd have some peace from him.'

It was too late: the whole company rejoined Justin who was found lying on his back behind the sofa beating his heels upon the wall.

His mother settled herself upon the sofa with the baby and tried to ignore him. There was a few minutes talk about the baby, increasingly interrupted by a banging sound from Justin and a muttered refrain which gradually became louder and louder.

'I don't like this house, don't like the furniture, don't like the people in it, it stinks and they stink too. Stink, stink!'

'Quiet, Justin,' said his father once or twice, from the depths of a talk about football with his brother.

Justin went on banging his heels, the women and Janice exclaimed over the baby and Linda and Peter were left to grimace at one another.

Then suddenly there was another noise in the room, another kind of muffled banging, *boom, boom, boom.*

Justin stopped his leg work and rolled on to his side.

'The wall banged back at me,' he said in a surprised voice. 'There it is again,' and again there came distinctly from the wall a muffled sound.

Boom, boom, boom.

'My goodness, Jim,' said Mrs Turner suddenly. 'It's our

new neighbours. That's the shared wall. Justin must have disturbed them.'

'This is fun,' cried Justin and banged again.

'Stop it, Justin!' cried his aunt.

He laughed and did it again.

'You mustn't shout at him like that if you don't mind,' said his mother, mottling over a little pinkly. 'I've always tried to be as reasonable as possible with him. Now, Justin, don't you see, you're disturbing the people who live next door to Aunt Jean and Uncle Jim.'

'Ha! Ha!' shouted Justin and drummed his heels as hard as they would go. He had at least taken his shoes off or the paint would have been damaged.

Boom, boom, boom, came back as a kind of echo.

'*Please* stop it, Justin,' cried Mrs Turner, getting up from the sofa.

He took not the slightest notice of her, so Peter went up to him and pulled him away from the wall.

He instantly began to howl, casting himself about on the floor and drumming his legs.

'A bit less reasoning and a good smack on his bottom is what he wants if you ask me,' said Mrs Turner grimly above the howls.

'We don't ask you, thank you,' snapped Aunty Sheila, her face now mottled as brightly pink as her dress. 'You'll allow me to know what's best for my own son. Now we'll have the devil's own time with him, calming him down. I shall probably be up half the night with him. And another time, Peter, I'll thank you to leave a little boy half your size alone.'

Peter looked at her. 'I was only – ' he began.

He saw his father shake his head at him, and stopped. It wasn't any good going on. Besides, no one was listening.

So he went quietly out of the room and, amazed at his own nobility, began to clear the dining room table, and so did not hear what went on in the sitting room and how it was all smoothed over. By the time all the plates were in the kitchen

Justin had stopped howling: there was a little more talk and then Peter heard them all saying goodbye in the hall.

Presently his mother and sisters came into the kitchen, and then his father, carrying the coffee cups.

'Oh dear, oh dear, I do wish I hadn't said that to Sheila,' Mrs Turner was saying. 'You know how she takes offence. But Justin is such an awful child and we can't let him go upsetting the Baxters.'

'Of course not,' agreed her husband. 'It was a bit unfortunate them knocking back like that, wasn't it? I've yet to speak to either of them. It's awkward if they're going to be difficult, isn't it?'

'Oh Jim,' said Mrs Turner, distractedly running water into the washing-up bowl, and squirting in too much soapy liquid. 'I don't know what to do about them and that's a fact. It's why I lost my temper with Justin like that. I'm afraid I've already upset them, and I didn't want any more trouble.'

Peter, Janice and Linda, each clutching a teacloth, stood silently waiting for knives and forks she was washing to emerge, and listening hard.

'It was earlier on this morning. You know that wind that got up, before it began to rain? Well, I had one or two things on the line, and a vest of Janice's came right off and blew over the hedge into the Baxters' garden. I could see it caught on the gooseberry bushes. The bush was so near our side I suppose I didn't think. I just popped through the gap in the hedge there, I was only in their garden a second, but of course it was trespassing, I ought really to have rung on their doorbell and asked but I didn't like to bother them, just for that. Well anyway, though I was only two paces into their garden, there she was, looking out of the window, and of course she saw me. So I sort of waved the vest as if to explain and thought no more of it, and that she would understand. But about ten minutes later, when I was putting the joint in, there was a ring at the door. It was him. And do you know what he said? He said to me, "Mrs Turner, I'll thank you not to keep on coming

27

in and out of our garden. You don't have free access any longer, whatever you seem to think," he said. Well I must admit I was rather taken aback and upset but of course I said that I was sorry and I ought to have knocked, and I tried to explain about the vest and he just grunted and said, "Well don't let it happen again," and stumped off. I didn't have time to tell you this earlier, Jim, I was in such a rush.'

'Oh I *say*, Mummy,' cried Janice. 'How horrid. Don't you think they are perfectly horrid, Dad?'

'I don't like the sound of that,' said her father slowly. 'If I were you, Jean, I wouldn't have anything to do with those two. After all, we don't want to have trouble, do we? Just keep out of their way, I should think that's best.'

'But now we've annoyed them even more with that awful Justin banging like that. Do you think it might smooth things over if I went and apologized? Though I can't say I want to meet *him* again very much. It might be easier if I could get her on her own sometime.'

'I don't expect you ever can,' commented Janice. 'They seem to be very much a pair, don't they? One telling the other, I mean. And they've only been out shopping once since they've been here, and that was together. He doesn't seem to go to work, does he? I don't think he ever leaves her on her own.'

''Course not, 'cos she's loony,' said Linda.

'Now children, that's enough of that. You're always to be polite to them if you meet them, and not to cause any trouble, do you hear?'

'Of course not,' remarked Janice virtuously, drying a glass and then looking through it. 'We're always polite. But suppose they're not polite to us? It *doesn't* take two to make a quarrel, you know. What about me and Sharon Davies at school? She just picks on me for nothing at all.'

'Grown-up people aren't like *children*,' said her little sister witheringly to her.

But here Janice had an unexpected ally in her mother.

28

'They can be, Linda,' she said, emptying the washing-up bowl, 'and that's what worries me. That's what worries me.'

It did not stop raining until after it was dark. Peter finished the book he was reading, got out of bed to turn out the light and draw back the curtains, and found a soft radiance bathing the garden from a three-quarter moon rising above the apple tree. Little rilled clouds were passing over the sky and through the moon so that it looked as if it were racing along and drawing the nearer stars after it. There was the low tweet twoot of an owl coming from the garden of Peacehaven or perhaps from a little farther off: from the tall elms in the meadow behind. It was answered on a deeper note from somewhere very close at hand to Peter. 'Twit-whoo, twit-who*o*' and the two owls kept up a kind of conversation together for a while. To Peter's excitement he thought he could make out the nearer owl sitting in an old apple tree not far from his bedroom window.

There were no lights in Peacehaven. Were they standing at their bedroom windows as he was, looking out at the moon-light garden and hearing the owls? Then a cow began bellowing from somewhere near the farm and Peter saw a large shape disengage itself from the apple tree and drift down the garden to be lost in the other fruit trees at the bottom, and then there were no further voices of any kind calling.

Later on in the night the moon moved to send its light on his pillow and he opened his eyes and realized he had been woken from a dream of owls: Mrs Baxter had become an owl, she had stood near the hedge and stared with two round owl eyes and then she had stretched her soft shapeless body into wings and rustled and flapped them, flap, flap, flap . . .

The next afternoon after school Peter was sitting upon the saddle of his bicycle which was leaning up against the front fence of Nut End. It was a pleasant afternoon, blue and cloudless, and he was idly wondering whether he was going to

29

bicycle up into the village or not – he had homework but he could do that any time – when his mother came up the front path from the house. 'Mr Baxter is scything down the grass at the bottom of his garden so I thought I'd take the opportunity to have a word with Mrs Baxter,' she said as she passed him.

'Oh.' A thrill of unpleasant anticipation went through Peter, he could not have explained why.

He remained sitting where he was and watched his mother knock at the front door of Peacehaven.

There was a pause, he could see the dark red curtain which was always half drawn across the front window twitch, and then at last the door opened a few inches.

'Oh, good afternoon, Mrs Baxter,' he could hear his mother say nervously. He then missed several sentences but guessed she was apologizing for Justin's bad behaviour the day before. It was evident that the explanation was being accepted because the door opened wider and Mrs Baxter advanced a pace or so. She was smiling. Now Peter could hear little snatches of the conversation.

'And is that your boy?'

'Yes, that's Peter. And I also have two girls, Janice and Linda – '

'Oh, yes. That's right.'

'I do hope they won't be a nuisance to you. I'm afraid children do make a bit of noise.'

'Oh, yes, that's right,' said Mrs Baxter again.

'I hope you've settled in nicely now, Mrs Baxter? The village is quite a friendly one really; there are various clubs and activities if you felt like joining anything.'

'Oh yes. I don't go out very much.'

'Is this part of the country strange to you, Mrs Baxter, or do you come from somewhere locally?'

'Yes, that's right, dear. We don't come from very far away. Not so very far away.'

'My husband's a local man,' said Peter's mother, making polite conversation. 'He and his brother were born in the village and his father before him and his grandfather before that. Not that Jim works here, of course. He has to drive into town. There's nothing much to do here unless you work on the land.'

'No, that's right,' agreed Mrs Baxter.

At that moment a woman with a basket over one arm and walking briskly and purposefully came down the road. It was Mrs Brown, one of the active women in the village who were always going about organizing people into doing things. She had an organizing look about her face now. She opened the gate of Peacehaven and walked up the path, waving cheerily to Peter's mother.

'Hullo, Jean. Good afternoon – Mrs Baxter, is it? I'm afraid I'm collecting again. Awful the way these collections come round and round isn't it. This one is for the blind.'

'I'll have to go back and get my bag,' said Peter's mother.

'Oh, I'll be coming round to you in a moment, Jean. Mrs Baxter, would you like to contribute a little something?'

She held up a collecting box and rattled it merrily, with an expectant laugh.

Mrs Baxter seemed a little taken aback. Her smile slowly left her face and she began to wipe one hand up and down on her dress.

'Oh, I don't know really, oh, here's my husband. Arthur, these ladies want me to give money for something they are collecting.'

The figure of Mr Baxter, looking rather hot and with shirt sleeves rolled up, appeared from behind his wife, pushing her to one side.

'We never give money on the doorstep. Anyway all these charities are rolling in money,' he said abruptly and crossly. 'Good afternoon.'

And the door of Peacehaven shut.

'*Oh,*' said Mrs Brown, momentarily rather daunted. 'Oh, well, never mind.'

'Come back to my house, Millie,' said Mrs Turner.

31

They walked back past Peter and down the path of Nut End.

'Come in a minute, Millie, won't you?' he heard his mother say.

When he himself went in a few minutes later he could hear animated conversation about the Baxters coming from their sitting room, the door of which was open.

'Oh dear, I can't help feeling a bit sorry for you,' he heard Mrs Brown exclaim in lively tones. 'Mrs Joyce was such a nice old thing. But what on earth are you stuck with now? Bad *luck*. He does seem a disagreeable man, doesn't he? Oh well, it takes all sorts to make a world, doesn't it?'

'Yes, I suppose it does. I can't help being a little apprehensive, Millie. You know how I hate unpleasantness of any kind. And Jim's just the same. He's never been one for making enemies.'

'Oh well, as long as you leave him strictly alone I expect he'll be all right. His wife seems pleasanter. But is she completely dominated by him?'

'I don't know. I'm beginning to wonder. If so, one ought to feel sorry for her, oughtn't one? What was that, Peter?' She came out into the hall. 'Why were you shouting "No!" like that?'

But she received no reply, for Peter was running up the stairs, two at a time. He did not know why he had shouted out, but he did know he did not want to talk or think about the Baxters any more.

4

The next day something good happened. Peter made a friend; or more precisely, a friendly acquaintance turned into a friend.

David Forster was one of the crowd who came some of the way back in Peter's coach, getting off at Pipers End. He was a chatty and popular boy in Peter's year, though not in the same form, and this was why they hadn't got to know each other earlier. But they were in the same English and French groups, and recently they had met again among those boys and girls who had been chosen to learn German. It was after a German lesson at the end of the afternoon that they began talking, were still talking when they got into the coach, were still talking when David decided to come all the way to Long Green with Peter and walk back the couple of miles home later on in the afternoon.

'If you've got a phone I could ring my mum and then she won't bother about me,' he said.

'Yes, that's O.K. You can ring from our place,' Peter assured him. It was delightfully flattering, that David should think him worth a two-mile walk.

'I expect Mum'll give you a cup of tea if you feel like it,' he said. 'Or we could get something from the shop. Anyway – '

'*Any*way,' David echoed. They looked at each other and grinned happily. The afternoon stretched ahead; golden and cloudless: no problems of any sort. They could do what they wanted to do. They would have a good time. No one can hurt you when you have a friend: together you can face the world and laugh at it.

'That's Peacehaven,' said Peter carelessly, sauntering past it. 'And a right nutty couple have just moved into it. Here's ours. Nut End.'

'Sounds the wrong way round,' commented David as they turned in at the open gate to Peter's house. 'If it's a nutty couple, *they* should live at Nut End and you at Peacehaven.'

'You're so right,' said Peter, struck with this. 'I'd better creep out in the middle of the night and change the names on the gates. Wonder how long it would take anybody to notice?'

And so altered and protected he felt by having his friend by him that the enormity of so doing did not strike him particularly: it seemed, for a little while anyway, a perfectly possible joke to play.

David was an appreciative companion. He liked Peter's house. He liked the fields at the back and the farm.

'Our house *is* in a village, I know,' he said. 'But it's just one of an estate, like all the rest. And they're all so beastly neat. My mum likes everything all easy and modern. And there are pavements and street lights. You might as well be in a town. The country's a bit boring round us too. I'd rather be up where there are hills and woods like you are.'

'It's not bad here,' admitted Peter, feeling a quite unexpected glow of pleasure and pride in his village. He had not looked at it like that before. It was just home. But he would not like to live at Pipers End: no, David was right, it was a dull featureless place, and too near the main road besides.

'Let's go down your garden,' suggested David after he had rung his mother and they had paused in the kitchen for a bite to eat, having had the most inadequate and dreadful school dinner imaginable.

'All right,' agreed Peter. 'Not that there's much to *do* there.'

But after a little wandering about and swinging on the branches of trees, they came upon a large multicoloured ball belonging to Linda and began idly kicking it to and fro.

'You keep goal between those two trees,' said David after a few minutes. He advanced towards Peter, dribbling the ball with great expertise and then launched an immense kick

34

upon it. It sailed effortlessly between the trees and above Peter's outstretched arms, on over the flower border and the hedge deep into the garden of Peacehaven.

'Oh bother,' exclaimed David, not realizing the enormity of what he had done. 'I was forgetting it was only a light ball. I can see it, can't you? It's over among some bushes, there.'

The ball's gay red and yellow stripes beckoned them from between the green foliage.

'Would they mind if I just nipped in and got it?' wondered David. 'I could slip through here very easily.'

'Better not.' A sense of dismay and foreboding filled Peter. If only he had had the sense not to start mucking about with Linda's ball like this. It was a new one; given to her by someone for her birthday not so very long ago. It would have to be retrieved or there would be trouble.

'Well, come on. Do we ask nicely at the front door then?'

'I suppose so.' A lot of Peter's carefree feelings about being now armed against the world and perhaps particularly the Baxters had evaporated. However, he steeled himself and together with David he marched resolutely up Peacehaven's path, trying not to notice the way the front curtain twitched as he passed it.

He knocked upon the door: it was the same knocker it had been in happier days, when they had popped round to Mrs Joyce on frequent errands and she had often invited them in and given them sweets. Silly how one remembered these little things.

It was a long time before anybody came, and they had time to raise their eyebrows and make faces at each other and then the door was opened a little way and Mr Baxter appeared, chewing at something, as if he had been interrupted in the middle of his tea.

'I'm very sorry,' said Peter as quickly and politely as he could, 'but I'm afraid our ball has gone over into your back garden. May we please go round and get it?'

Mr Baxter swallowed and then brought out a large greyish handkerchief and began slowly to wipe his hands with it. His face began to redden as he stared at each one of them.

'You'll do no such thing,' he said loudly at last. 'Indeed you'll do no such thing. Smashing down the garden with balls, is it now? Well, the ball can just lay there and rot for all I care.'

And he thrust his face towards Peter as he said this and then slammed the door.

The boys walked back up the path in stunned silence. For a few minutes they could not think what to do. They wandered down the garden again and stared through the hedge at the ball, so near and yet so far.

'You know I could be through and back in a second,' said David, measuring the distance with his eye.

'No, don't!' Peter pulled him back.

'Why not?'

'Don't you see? Look, *she's* there.'

And there, standing near the ball, half behind a tree, looking towards them, was Mrs Baxter.

'Nutty as a fruit cake,' was David's comment. And then he thought of something else to do and Peter did not blame him for it; it was not his problem.

Soon he had to go, and Peter went some of the way with him and talked about adventure stories and science fiction, quite forgetting Linda and her ball.

But when he came home there were she and Janice down the garden, looking through the hedge at it.

'You've gone and lost my ball now!' were Linda's first furious words. 'When we'd stopped looking at Blue Peter we went out for a game and that's where we saw it!'

'You and your *friend*,' added Janice with withering scorn. 'And I suppose Mr Baxter won't let you have it back.'

'I'm sorry. No, he won't,' muttered Peter weakly. 'We did ask.'

'But I can't lose my ball just like that!' wailed Linda, the enormity of it suddenly striking her. 'I shall tell Mummy.'

And so she did: but her mother was not much help. 'I don't know I'm sure,' she said once or twice. 'Well, I'm too busy now anyway, getting Daddy's tea. I don't like to bother them again and that's a fact.'

'I shall ask Daddy to get it for me when he comes back,' sniffed Linda.

But when Mr Turner came back he was in a hurry for his tea because he had to go out again to a committee meeting of the cricket club of which he was a keen member.

'Oh, leave the ball,' he said on hearing the whole story. 'If they want to act unpleasant, let them. I'll get you another, Linda.'

'But – ' began Linda tearfully.

'Not another word, do you hear? I'll get you another,' he said loudly.

Something had obviously made him rather cross: when this happened, and it was not often, his children had learnt to keep their peace. So the meal ended in silence.

Peter then went upstairs and tried to settle to an hour's homework. But a face kept coming between him and his geography book. A furious face, with a little bristling moustache. And because he had been really near to it for the first time since – for the first time – this face had something upon its forehead which he had not previously noticed.

A wart. The forehead had a wart, in the middle, between the eyebrows. There was now no possible escape, and Peter realized that he had been subconsciously trying to escape.

The couple next door bore exactly the same features and bodies as the sinister couple he had awoken in the wood. It had not been a dream. Or if it had been a dream it was a dream that was still being dreamt.

And so what was going to happen next?

5

Quite suddenly the holidays arrived. It was nearly the end of July. Peter had one enjoyable day at David's home and returned to a lull in his own affairs. David was going away the next day. Half the village seemed to be going away. Peter and his family would be visiting relatives in Plymouth soon: meanwhile time slowed.

'What are you doing today, Peter?' said his mother at about twelve o'clock one morning. 'Aren't you going out? What about your car-cleaning job? Or jobs for me? If you want to stay in your room you might at least make the bed and tidy it. Don't sigh at me like that, there's a good boy. Shoes! Do put your shoes on, not leave them for me to fall over in the doorway.'

Driven from his refuge by her energy he wandered out on to the landing. He could hear a shrill murmur of femininity pervading the house: Linda and her friend were closeted in the bathroom from which muffled shrieks, splashes and giggles could be heard; they were washing their dress-up dolls and the greater part of their dolls' wardrobes. From the girls' room came more voices and the wails of a pop singer: Janice entertaining two of *her* friends. They had to shout to make themselves heard above the pop music and snatches of what they were saying penetrated, although the door was shut.

'I don't like *her* do you Janice: not after what she said to Lesleyanne James when I said I liked Lesleyanne's hair the new way her mum had cut it: well, *she* said . . . and then *I* said . . .'

Another voice took up the theme, speaking excitedly and interrupting the first speaker.

'No; well do you know what I said to *her*? Do you know?

38

What I said to her? Are you listening? Oh Janice, do shut *up*, I want to tell Shirley what I said – '

Females! Yatter, yatter, *yuk*.

Peter wandered in slow motion into the kitchen where he would have helped himself from the biscuit tin had there been any biscuits left in it. He sighed deeply once or twice.

Presently there was a thunder of feet down the stairs and girlish voices at the front door:

'Goodbye, Anne, goodbye, Shirley, see you tomorrow. Goodbye,' and then a silence and then Janice wandered a little disconsolately and loose-endishly into the kitchen.

'Their mum is taking them shopping in the car,' she said. 'I wish *our* mum drove and had a car of her own.'

'She did have driving lessons once,' said Peter. 'It wasn't her fault she wasn't much good at it.'

'*I* think she was *silly* to be so nervous,' said Janice pettishly.

'You leave Mum out of it. You can't help how you're made.'

'*I* shall be an extremely good driver when I get my sports car when I'm a famous model.'

'*You* – a famous *what*? You'll be a famous lump of suet pudding with a frill round its middle,' mocked her brother, unfairly, because Janice was solidly built but not in the least fat.

'Oh shut up! You're always getting at me and I hate you,' she replied with spirit.

Because they were bored and irritated each other with their boredom, they worked up quite a good and noisy quarrel. It must have sounded a good deal worse than they really meant, because both were surprised by their mother coming into the kitchen looking distraught and calling out in a desperate voice.

'Oh, for goodness sake do stop it you two or I shall be driven out of my mind! It's quite enough to have Linda and Mandy messing up the bathroom, and at least *they*'re nice to one another. You ought to be ashamed of yourselves. It's a lovely day. Why on earth don't you both go out? Go out together for a change. I'll make you some sandwiches if you like and you can buy a bottle of pop down the village and go for a picnic.'

'Peter wouldn't want to go out with me,' muttered Janice, but at the same time a glimmer of something approaching hope came into her face.

'Well, if he doesn't he's a very unpleasant boy and a bad brother to you. Now come on Peter, try being nice to Janice for a change.'

'Me! Nice for a change! How about her?' he began hotly, but then stopped, feeling ashamed. 'I don't mind going out for a picnic,' he said at length.

'All right, that's settled then,' his mother said quickly. 'And I'll give you some money for your drinks and perhaps some crisps as well. Take a watch, one of you – I want you back soon after five at the latest.'

'We could pack the picnic in my satchel,' cried Janice eagerly. She ran to get it, with joy and pleasure in her face.

'You see, your sister really loves to be with you,' said Mrs Turner when Janice had gone. 'It's a pity you can't get together more often.'

'Well I don't mind, but why is she so beastly to me just about all the time?' protested Peter, both ashamed and yet also aggrieved. 'She doesn't let me alone. I've always got to be taking notice of her.'

His mother made no reply but sighed deeply as she began to cut and butter bread.

'Not jam, cheese, please,' he put in anxiously. 'And can we take some apples?'

Ten minutes later he and Janice wandered up the village street together towards the shop. They had made no plans as to where to go: both were now a little silent and sulky with one another, and Peter half knew that he was the only one who could alter this state of affairs: if he gave Janice any encouragement she would chat away happily and then they could think where to go and their expedition might be a success, but somehow he couldn't quite manage this.

40

The old grey Morris which he recognized as belonging to the Baxters was parked outside the village shop, and as he and Janice approached the door it opened and both Mr and Mrs Baxter came out, she following behind her husband as she always did. It gave Peter a little shock, as he had never met them outside the boundaries of Peacehaven, but they took no notice of him and got into their car and drove away. It was all over in a matter of seconds. Peter and Janice went into the shop and began looking among the bottles of ginger beer and limeade.

There was a slight cessation of a murmured conversation as they went into the shop, and he had the impression that Mr and Mrs Baxter were being discussed by the two middle-aged women already in the shop.

'If we have these two bottles, limeade and cherryade,' began Janice, 'and a small bag of crisps we've just enough left for a toffee bar, do let's, Peter.'

'O.K.'

They paid, and left the shop.

'Come on,' said Peter briskly. 'Just follow me. *I* know where we're going.'

'All right, Peter.'

And Janice began to sing as she skipped along beside him.

'Oh for goodness sake, we must have walked *miles*. Do let's have our picnic now.'

'Just a little further,' said Peter relentlessly. He wanted to get to the wood at least.

Janice's face was pink and sweaty. She limped slightly and was obviously tired, hot, and over-ready for her lunch. It was a marvel she hadn't complained before this, knowing her.

'You've done very well,' he said to encourage her. 'Do you see those trees up there? It's a wood and it'll be all cool and mossy inside.'

'All right. I'm absolutely longing for a drink.'

'And we'll have one, just in a few minutes – '

41

They went on, Peter privately congratulating himself on the way he was handling her. Why, it was not so very difficult after all. She had been quite pleasant company, in fact. And it would be a good thing to have someone with him for later, for a witness.

They entered the little wood. Now they had got there, Peter was ready for Janice to sink down anywhere and demand her lunch, but she wandered on, down the path to where it came to a natural halt in the clearing where the stones had been uncovered.

It looked just the same: dimly lit by shafts of sunlight striking down between the trees, quietly awaiting them. There were no signs that anybody had been there since Peter's last visit.

'What was here?' exclaimed Janice curiously. 'Do you think there was a house once? It looks like a bit of wall, doesn't it? Ooh, it's creepy here, isn't it?'

If she stopped talking, they could have heard the humming almost-silence, but she did not.

'What's down there?' she went on, plunging down a bank. 'Look at the enormous rabbit holes.'

Peter had not noticed these before. 'Badger perhaps,' he said, coming down to them. They both bent and peered inside but could see nothing except earth and roots and a few dried leaves.

'We might find badger droppings,' exclaimed Janice excitedly. 'What do they look like, Pete?'

'Search me,' he said, wondering himself. 'Bigger than rabbits', I suppose.'

'Oh, mind those beastly midges. Do you see that great cloud of them? Let's have our food over there, by the big tree, right at the edge and look out over the fields ahead. Come on.'

So they did as she suggested and soon felt a good deal better. They ate and drank everything until it was all gone and then Janice put all the pieces of paper and the two empty bottles back into the satchel. The wood at their backs was just an ordinary wood now. It was good to think of badgers living there, tunnelling under the ruins of whatever building it had been.

'Fancy having a house in the middle of a dark wood,' said Janice then, as if she had been listening to Peter's thoughts.

Something stirred way back in Peter's mind. 'Perhaps there wasn't a wood then,' he said uncertainly.

'Don't be silly. There must have been. Some of those oak trees are awfully old, even if the little trees and things could have come up later. Oak trees can grow for three hundred or four hundred years.'

'Ruins can be older still,' he said, but vaguely. The wood itself seemed so ancient, so permanent, he couldn't think back beyond it. He was tired, and full of food, and they had farther to go.

'Come on.' He got up.

'You're not going on any *more*,' she exclaimed. 'Remember we've got to walk all the way back again. Unless you're taking me round in a circle?'

'No, I don't think so, though there probably is a shorter way home. Come on, Janice. It's nice over that field and up again through the next lot of trees. It honestly is rather interesting. You'll like it when you get there.'

'All right,' she said doubtfully, but trusting him. 'Get where? Where is it we are going to get?'

Where indeed? Now they were so near his heart began to thump and he felt his breath coming unevenly. They walked over the next field which bore the traces of having contained cows in the not so very distant past: clouds of flies rose from aged cow pats and the field had a soiled, trampled look. An aeroplane went over, a large, noisy jet, and somewhere there was the continued whine of a mechanical saw.

'It's not quite like it was,' muttered Peter half to himself, uncertainly. But he recognized the field, the wide ditch over which they had to jump, the series of little rough pasture fields which came next, one leading out of the other. The fields

43

narrowed on either side of them until they were walking down a wide path contained by high hedges. There was a stile and a signpost saying 'Fairfield Green, one mile.'

'Wait,' began Peter, puzzled. He looked back: where had he gone wrong? Was there another path through those neglected patches of teasel and bramble? He walked back a few paces. There were several large oak trees, both standing in the fields and in the hedgerows: there was a jumble of lesser trees, bushes and nettles, but no large wood and no path leading to one. Once before, it had been like the outer arms of a forest stretching out with the feeling of more, much more beyond. But looking back and to either side now he could see that it was all broken up into little fields and hedgerows. It looked wooded from a distance, but it wasn't really. About a quarter of a mile away in one direction he caught sight of telegraph posts and wire; obviously a road of some sort lay concealed there. The normal twentieth-century world was hemming them in too closely: there simply wasn't *room*.

'What's the matter?' asked Janice. 'Have you lost the way?'

'Yes. Sort of. It's all gone different. It *was* the same, and now it isn't. I don't see where I went wrong. I don't understand it,' he said desperately.

'You've been here before then? Where *are* we anyway? What are you trying to find?' she asked impatiently.

'Oh, I can't possibly explain,' he began crossly, but then paused, because he had to speak about it to somebody. And then, as if an obstruction within himself had broken, he found himself seated on the rough grass by the stile and the signpost which said 'Fairfield Green one mile' and beginning to tell her all about it: how his walk a few weeks ago had become odder and odder and how it had been more and more frightening as well, and how he had awoken the couple in the wood.

'And it was when I saw the wart on his face the other day I *knew*,' he ended up. 'I knew it was Mr Baxter. If I dreamt them before I met them it was the most real dream I've ever had in my life.'

44

'Golly, Pete!' He could see a variety of thoughts and emotions chasing themselves across Janice's face. 'Of course you went into a tree or something *before* the country started going queer,' she said at last with authority. 'You were sort of knocked half asleep. And then you fell right asleep and dreamt a dream properly. People do dream about people before meeting them, you know. I read it in a book, there was some story – '

'Yes, in *stories*,' put in Peter. 'But this is real life. The Baxters are really there.'

'It's really the opposite of "The Sleeping Beauty",' continued Janice thoughtfully. 'The Sleeping Uglies. And two of them. You didn't wake them with a kiss, you woke them, him anyway with a *kick*, by stumbling on to him, didn't you?'

'And then he kicked *her*,' said Peter, remembering and shuddering.

'It *must* have been a nasty dream.'

'I suppose you're right,' he said thoughtfully after a pause. 'It *was* a dream of course, as I thought at first, and then I thought it couldn't be, and then I thought – oh, I don't know. It's been so confusing. I've had these awful feelings about them, I don't understand it.'

'Well, so've I,' said Janice reasonably. 'They're awful people. Creepy. I'm afraid of what they're going to do to us.'

At her echoing so closely yet more rationally his own fears, Peter perversely enough began to cheer up. He now saw that it had been very comforting to come here and to find it just ordinary, and to tell somebody about it. She believed him in the only sense that mattered: that the Baxters held some significance for them, for their family. She accepted this without question. He was glad he had told her: the telling of it all reduced it. Anything else, any other doubt or fear he pushed to the very back of his mind and was glad to keep it there.

'You know, I think I've heard of Fairfield Green,' said Janice thoughtfully. 'Let's go on and find a road and I bet we can come home a shorter way.'

And so that was what they did: Fairfield Green proved only to be a few houses round a rough triangle of grass, but there was another signpost at a small crossroads and one arm pointed to Hartshorn. Hartshorn apparently was two miles away and Hartshorn was a village they both knew: it could indeed be called a neighbouring village to their own village. The road was the obvious way back. Soon they must reach familiar territory.

Like all supposedly short ways it took longer to walk than they had thought and it was close on five o'clock by the time they turned into their own familiar road. Their legs ached and they were hungry and thirsty all over again.

The milkman was at Peacehaven's front door as they passed it; he was on his usual Friday afternoon rounds collecting the week's money. Dimly they heard his voice and Mrs Baxter's:

'And another five pence – '

'That'll do fine. Thank *you*. Good afternoon to you.'

''Afternoon.'

Rattle, clink as he moved his van on. Now coming down their path just behind them.

'Afternoon,' to their mother who appeared at the door. 'Eighty-six, please – '

His demeanour with them, with the Baxters, was so normal, so commonplace. He had not the air of one coming from a house of foul fiends: real, or summoned up in nightmare. He had the carefree air of a man all of whose customers paid their bills cheerfully, said 'Good afternoon', were normal, rational beings. 'Sleeping Uglies': was there anything so ridiculously unlikely?

'*Thank* you. Bye, bye.'

For some reason Peter was immensely comforted by the milkman.

'Well, you've been out a good long time,' their mother welcomed them.

'We've been miles and miles; the longest walk I've ever walked,' cried Janice.

'Come on in and I'll make you a nice cup of tea.'

They went inside to the cool comfort of their home and the door closed behind them.

6

'Goodness me, the Mayhews are having their house painted at last!' exclaimed Mrs Turner.

'It's about time,' commented her husband.

'That'll brighten the village up,' said Janice. 'Mum! Do you see? There must have been a big storm sometime! The top half of the big old elm tree is down, the elm tree at the corner. Look!'

Everybody craned their necks to see.

'I should think some of that must've fallen across the road,' exclaimed Peter. 'I wonder if anybody was passing underneath?'

'Look!' screamed Linda suddenly, startling them all. 'There's Lucinda Bradbrook!' She waved enthusiastically. 'She's waving to me!'

'So what, there's Lucinda Bradbrook,' sniffed Janice crushingly. 'So what's so wonderful about that?'

But then she caught sight of one of her own friends just coming out of the village shop.

'There's Anne,' she could not stop herself saying.

'And there's Anne's *dog* tied to the railings waiting for her and there's Anne's mother and baby brother too,' Peter mocked her, though he understood her excitement. It *was* exciting and very pleasant coming home after a fortnight's absence. They only went away for a long break like that once a year and there was time for all sorts of little changes to have happened in the village, and for the old familiar surroundings to have taken on a just slightly different look. It was fun to go away, right away to a different part of England, where the whole lie of the land was altered, and to see the sea, but how comforting it was to come back to their own little landlocked

48

piece of country whose woods and gently rising hills and varied fields nestled about them with such gentle and homely pleasure to the eye.

'East, west, home's best,' said their mother, turning round and smiling at them from the front of the car.

'And here we are!'

Peacehaven and Nut End greeted them, bathed in sunlight, surrounded with greenery.

'My word, *look* at that grass. It's knee high almost!'

'The hollyhocks are nearly all out.'

'Where did those snapdragons come from? I'd never noticed them there before.'

'I wonder if Mrs Mills had time to come and pick those plums for me, as she promised?'

Nobody was listening to anybody else. The children flung themselves out of the car and ran round the side of the house to the back, too impatient to wait for their parents, struggling with suitcases and the front door key.

And it was then that they saw it. When they were in the back garden, outside the locked kitchen door.

A barbed wire fence with several thick strands and many posts now separated their garden from Peacehaven's. It had been put in on *their* side of the hedge in some places; in others, where the hedge had been thin it was now half destroyed and the wire fence trampled it heedlessly down. It was raw, crude and aggressive. It spoiled the pleasant completeness of the two gardens, which needed each other as the two halves of the same picture need one another. Now an ugly line had been slashed right across the middle of this picture, contemptuously desecrating it, ruining it. But it was what the line proclaimed that was the truly worrying and dreadful thing.

The three of them stood rooted to the ground in shock for several seconds.

Then Linda called out 'Mummy! Daddy! Look what's happened!' and ran back to fetch them, by which time of course they had let themselves into the front of the house and had reached the kitchen and scullery, were unbolting the back door and could see for themselves.

'Well I'm damned!' said their father, slowly coming outside, the pleasure of homecoming gradually draining from his face and being replaced by something quite different. He then, under his breath, said some very much worse words than 'damn'. Peter, who heard them, sympathized with him, yet was a little shocked. He didn't think his father should know such words. It was all right for the boys at school, but fathers should really have a little more self-control.

His mother came out to stand beside them. 'But they can't!' she exclaimed helplessly. 'What will Miss Joyce say? You can't behave like that in rented property.'

'No you damn well can't and they're well over the boundary line in places, look there, and *there*.'

Linda had gone inside the house but the rest of the family walked down the garden to see the extent of the damage. Many plants and bushes on the borderline were smashed and trodden down, and at the bottom, where there was only one old rickety piece of wooden fencing between their orchard and the fields beyond, they found the wire now excluding a piece of land they had always regarded as their own: their rhubarb patch. Admittedly the hedge was almost non-existent down here and the general line of it had wandered somewhat – but those few feet had always been their rhubarb patch and Mrs Joyce had not objected. She had had her own rhubarb on the other side of her garden, loads of it. There was always more rhubarb than one needed anyway, once the stems grew long and tough. Now they were cut off by wire from their own rhubarb which they had eaten in pies and crumbles early in summer every year without fail.

Janice pointed at it in silence. There was no need to say anything.

'Right. I'm going round to sort this out just as soon as I've washed and put the car away,' said Mr Turner grimly, turning on his heel and striding back up the garden. The others followed him more slowly, all three of them casting surreptitious glances over into the next door garden to see if the Baxters were watching.

But for once there was no sign of them. Their windows were closed: there was no peering face. Near the house they were able to breathe a sigh of relief because Nut End and Peacehaven were so arranged that both the back and front doors were some distance apart at opposite sides of the two houses and so, for a semi-detached, there was a fair amount of privacy: also the number of shrubs and large bushes growing on either side of the boundary near the houses gave further protection.

Peter and Janice followed each other inside in silence. Then Peter took his suitcase which had been brought into the hall and ran hastily upstairs with it to his room and shut the door. He had this awful feeling he was going to break down and cry. He wanted to cry badly, and he wanted to shout and kick and swear.

The fence looked just as bad from his bedroom window, worse if anything.

He had had a good holiday; he had truly forgotten the Baxters, or if they had passed through his mind at all he had dismissed them as unimportant; he had been so happy returning through the village, resolved to ignore them and get on with his own affairs – and now it was impossible. They did not want to be ignored, and that was the truth of it. Well, he was not *going* to allow them to spoil things. He would not give them any further thought, so there. He had been caught by surprise this time, but never again. He did not give a damn about the whole business, not he. Tomorrow he would ring David and see if he were back. He would look out one or two of his mates down the village. They would be bored by now and quite ready to make friends again. He would earn a little money by cleaning his old friend Miss Armitage's car within the next day or so; his mother was right, he had not been there for ages. She might be after another boy if he didn't turn up soon.

Those were the things he would do, and to hell with the whole world.

7

'Yes, well, and then Linda's ball went over and we never got it back. But that's all right because Dad got her another, a great big beach ball, while we were away on holiday,' said Peter cheerfully, taking another large bite of cake.

'Oh dear, dear, deary me,' commented Miss Armitage, also cheerfully, wedging her large behind more securely into the seat of her windsor chair. It was the morning after Peter's return from holiday: he had cleaned Miss Armitage's car for her and now he was being rewarded with coffee and cake in her kitchen. The financial side of the reward already lay pleasantly heavy in his trouser pocket. As usual, for such car cleaning mornings, they were deep in the middle of one of their chats. Miss Armitage was a very easy woman to talk to, at least Peter thought her so; in many ways considerably easier than his parents; and he found himself telling her all sorts of things.

'But you say something worse than that happened,' prompted Miss Armitage after a few seconds. '*Down*, Bunty.'

Bunty, a Sealyham bitch, subsided to the floor, her eyes riveted on the piece of cake in Miss Armitage's large, not over-clean hand. Two other Sealyhams regarded her and Peter from strategic positions upon the floor. A cat (one of five) weaved its way along the kitchen table between the coffee pot, the milk jug and the plate of cakes.

'Now they've gone and put in a barbed wire fence right down the back garden,' continued Peter. 'And there wasn't half a bust up between Mr Baxter and Dad about it afterwards.'

He laughed, but it was nearly a shudder. It had been far from funny when his father had come walking away from the

Baxters' house, his hands thrust deep in his pockets, his face red with anger.

'I don't want to discuss it,' he had said, the moment he got inside his own house and met his family's inquiring eyes. 'I'm putting it in the hands of my solicitors. That's what I told him when he wouldn't listen to reason and started pouring out all sorts of nonsense. I shall simply put it in the hands of my solicitors.'

'Gracious, Daddy!' exclaimed Janice in all innocence. 'Do you *have* any solicitors?'

Poor Janice! She blushed red, near to tears, as her father crushingly told her not to stick her oar in where it was not wanted nor meddle with things she did not understand. Then he took their mother by the arm and led her into the sitting room, shutting the door in their faces.

'I didn't know Daddy knew any solicitors,' muttered Janice, her feelings very wounded because as the elder girl her father often made much of her.

'I don't think it's quite like that,' said Peter to her, from his two years' senior knowledge of the world and its ways. 'You just go to the nearest town that has a firm of solicitors and ask them to do a job for you. You don't need to know them personally or to have used them before or anything like that.'

'Solicitors, eh,' said Miss Armitage thoughtfully. '*Down*, Bunty. It's a pity when it comes to that between neighbours, but I know very well how these things can happen in a village. It's a very tricky business having neighbours, isn't it? I'm sure in your case you've been very unlucky. I've heard one or two not very good things about these Baxters already. I believe they've already started on the other side – on Mr North and his goat. They say the goat has been eating their hedge or something. And that it smells and they're going to call the R.S.P.C.A. in or such nonsense. Poor old Mr North was quite upset. You know how he looks after everything so beautifully. And he does such a good job for me too, trimming my hedges and helping me with the veg.'

54

'I didn't know they'd started on Mr North,' exclaimed Peter. He stirred his cup and looked about Miss Armitage's kitchen. Of course Miss Armitage herself didn't actually have neighbours; not in the close-living sense of the word. For the first time he thought of her as lucky, instead of funny old Miss Armitage who had known his father as a boy and had lived in this nice redbrick house with white shutters and a big garden all her life.

Miss Armitage was the daughter of a retired admiral. Peter could just remember old Admiral Armitage and had heard many a story of the way he had thrown his weight about in the village and been chairman of the Parish Council and this and that. Nobody had liked him very much, but Peter's grandfather many many years ago had been Admiral Armitage's gardener. Peter's father often told stories about how Grandad had got up and left the room or the pub or wherever he was when anybody spoke too badly of the Admiral, though he would criticize him sometimes himself, in the privacy of his own home.

'But Miss Armitage, she's all right,' Peter's father would end up saying. 'She was very kind to me and Ron. She helped us both get to the Grammar School, of that I'm sure, with all the extra time she spent talking to us and coaching us. You just make certain you mind your manners when you speak to her, Peter. I know some of the village people laugh at her now she's let herself go and got all those animals and doesn't care what she says or how she looks, but they've got short memories some of them. There's no point in knocking people like her: she's got a lot more to her than some of this new lot of people flooding into the village: nothing to them at all, some of them, however they might speak and whatever they might think themselves to be.'

A long and interesting speech which had shed little lights of illumination in Peter's mind and led him to think up questions he would have liked to ask, but somehow the opportunity went by and he never did.

Miss Armitage unwedged herself from her chair and stood up. 'I'm so sorry your parents are bothered by these horrible people,' she said briskly. 'From what I know of your mother it's the sort of thing that would upset her very much. She's a sensitive little thing, isn't she? I always think neighbour trouble is worse for the woman in the home than for the husband who gets away from it by going out to work. Come into the sitting room for a moment if you've finished your coffee. I've an old book I want to lend your father, if I can lay my hands on it.'

So Peter accompanied by all three dogs followed her into the sitting room which was large and rather cold after the kitchen: it had a lot of china in various cupboards and good-looking furniture, mostly hidden by piles of books, photographs, knitting and cats. Recumbent cat bodies indeed lay curled in all the most comfortable chairs. There were dog hairs all over the carpet which didn't look as if it had been swept for some time.

Miss Armitage looked vaguely about the room. 'Now where did I put it? It's just a book of old reminiscences of this part of the country and there's a Turner mentioned several times as living in this village. I think it must have been some relative of yours. I know your family has been living here for generations, hasn't it? Look on the window sill for me, there's a good chap. It could be in that pile there.'

Peter picked his way across the floor, avoiding a large, gravy-stained dinner plate near the sofa – whether the remains of some animal banquet or Miss Armitage's own dinner he had no means of telling – and stumbling over a wastepaper basket lying on its side with all its papers spilling out of it.

'Tut, tut,' remarked Miss Armitage at this juncture. 'Dratted cats had the basket over again.'

'This it?' asked Peter doubtfully, after turning over the dusty pile of books.

'That's the one. Well done. Take it home with you, would you? Your father can let me have it back any time.'

A piece of paper floated out as Peter tucked the book under his arm.

'Does this belong?' he asked.

'Now what's that? Ah yes. That's a bit of an old local ballad I found in the book and copied out because it might have a bearing on a character I'm interested in. Like to have a look?'

More out of politeness than because he was interested Peter took the paper back from her and read:

'Sir Robert was as true a knight
As ever smote with sword
Yet swore he ne'er no more to fight
But pray within the wood.

His armour stout he cast aside
His horse he gave away
He dwelt within the greenwoods wide
Spake with wild beasts each day.

He dared to do what no man could
He laid the monsters in their lair
With sleep as white as any a cloud
To be their blanket evermore.'

'Fascinating, isn't it?' said Miss Armitage when he handed the paper back to her. 'It looks as if there should have been more verses between the second and the last. We ought to have heard more about those monsters, oughtn't we? And heaven knows when it was written: if early on, I mean sometime between fourteen and fifteen hundred or so, the spelling would have been different. I suppose somebody could have changed it later on, some editor or other. The poem's of no literary value, I suppose. But the chap I'm interested in was known as Robert the Hermit: he lived sometime in the thirteen hundreds and apparently was widely known as a wise man and healer. He could have been a knight first. It's difficult to pin down exactly where he lived but anyway it was north of Hertford and considerably south of Cambridge. Not on or near Royston Heath I don't think; he would have been south west, somewhere in the woods. Of course the forests were vast in those days: there were only a few villages and clearings and the occasional track or Roman road through.'

'Yes,' said Peter, and a strange shiver ran down his back. Robert the Hermit. Great forests, little clearings . . .

'I suppose as you're interested in old things you don't know anything about some very old ruins about four or five miles from here in a wood?' he suddenly plucked up courage to ask her. 'It's difficult to explain exactly where they are, but it looked as if someone had been digging them up a bit recently, and if you go on for about another twenty minutes you come to a sign post and then to Fairfield Green.'

'Oh, Fairfield Green. Yes. As a matter of fact I took a part in that dig though I'm a bit on the ancient side for such hard work. There are a lot of badger holes underneath too, and the site's not an easy one. Got bitten alive by mosquitoes, it was oppressive and stuffy and – well, there didn't seem the enthusiasm there ought to have been for it. People began to drop out. Then I dropped out. I don't think they – I'm referring to the Archaeological Society of course – went much further on after that, not after they'd found out what it obviously was.'

'And what was it?' Peter asked, as casually as he could.

'Oh, the foundations of a twelfth-century manor house, without doubt. The proportions were just right. The funny thing is that it's such a long way from anything like a village – unless there was one which disappeared. I must walk round there again with the dogs one day. But it's not a part of the country I like, for some reason. Bad farmers, neglected land – I don't know. A bit of a mess, as I remember. It was somewhere round there that Bunty and Sausage got themselves caught up on really vicious barbed wire and I went to rescue them and found my leg in one of those beastly snare traps. *Not* good walking.'

Miss Armitage sniffed loudly, dismissing the whole district and wiping her nose with the back of her hand in just the sort of way Peter's mother had expressly forbidden him to do.

'I'd better be getting back,' he exclaimed, remembering

58

that it would be a meal time. He was glad of the excuse: Miss Armitage's house, pleasant as it was, and Miss Armitage's strong personality dominating it; the clouds of cigarette smoke now surrounding her, the short vigorous growth of iron grey hair bushing about her head, her cats and her dogs, all these things together became too strong for Peter as they had sometimes before and he wanted to get away.

'See you next week. Cheerio.'

'Goodbye.'

As usual, she did not accompany him to the door and so he saw himself out past the flower prints in the hall, past the old grandfather clock always ticking but always showing the wrong time, to the front door.

'Your post's come, Miss Armitage,' he called, seeing it on the mat.

'Oh let it lie there, it'll only be bills, nobody writes to me now,' she bellowed back cheerily.

Certainly the envelopes were all buff.

And then he was outside. Robert the Hermit. The words had such a familiar sound but where could he have heard them?

Peter took the field north from Miss Armitage's house, the one which approached the church which was set high on a hill overlooking the village. It was a Norman church with a tall spire which could be seen for many miles around. Because it was an old church it needed a great many repairs: Peter knew that something to do with retiling the spire was going to take place, and there had also been talk about the clock, the face of the clock to be cleaned or some such enterprise. Nevertheless it was a shock to him when he saw the clock face now in view some two hundred yards ahead of him begin to lurch to one side and then slowly descend to the ground, because he was too far away to easily make out the ropes and pulleys which must lie behind this feat of engineering.

'They're taking the face off Time, aren't they?' said a voice behind him, startling him considerably. It was only talkative little Miss Battcock, come up while he had been stock still and staring. 'In a manner of speaking. Leaves quite a hole doesn't it,' she went on, referring to the now complete absence of the clock face. 'The church doesn't seem right without it.'

'No,' agreed Peter, and he walked on behind her until he could plainly see the large clock face now stationary at the foot of the church tower, and the couple of men who had moved it. He would have liked to linger, but he was already late for his dinner.

Nothing else happened that day except for the slight feeling of fullness Peter was conscious of from time to time. This was not a physical fullness as if he had had a particularly large dinner, but a kind of mental fullness – as if something interesting had happened to him and he wanted to think about it but for the life of him he could not think what the interesting thing could be. He went to bed early that night, there being nothing particular on the television, and very soon was asleep.

'They're taking the face off Time' clanged a voice somewhere deep within Peter's dream. He turned to lie on his back, his mouth open as images of great clocks pressed down on him, to be somehow replaced by marching, shuffling feet, thousands and thousands of them: men and animals trampling on and on – great plough horses and oxen pulled enormous carts and wagons, raising vast clouds of dust, and Peter as he watched them pass realized that he was standing by the verge of a road which wound up and down and on and on over bare, grassy hills. It was twilight and slowly the multitudes of people thronged by until he found himself alone on the hillside in the near dark. And then far off in the emptiness there came one solitary figure walking along the greyish stony road. As it drew nearer and nearer he could see it was a very tall man; not young, because his white hair fluttered about his forehead. He was partially dressed in armour; as he approached, Peter saw that he was holding a great sword stained near the tip with

blood. Suddenly, with a convulsive gesture, the tall man threw his sword far away behind him so that it spun over and over, its steel finally hitting the stony road with a resounding clatter. He was muttering and talking to himself and continuing to take off pieces of his armour and cast them away.

He drew level with Peter, who realized the height and breadth of the man; though he was growing old and shambled a little, limping every now and then for a pace or so, he appeared a formidable figure with much power still in his massive shoulders, his long arms and hands. His expression was open, kindly, his grey beard thinnish and straggly, his eyes, a soft, pale blue, glanced about him mildly, until he chanced to look up to the far distant rim of the hills when they froze and glared as if he saw a vision. As he walked on, now passing Peter, it became apparent through the dusk that there were a growing number of children and animals following behind him; then a little girl bolder than the rest ran up and caught him by the hand, birds fluttered out of nowhere to circle his head and dogs and donkeys trotted meekly behind, their eyes fixed upon him.

On and on he strode, his white hair continuing to shine out in the darkness long after his looming figure and the figures of his little procession were lost from view, leaving nothing behind but the dying patter of many feet, like the rustle of dried leaves turning over in the breath of a gentle wind.

The leaves in the tree outside Peter's open window moved and sighed and he opened his eyes.

'I have seen Robert the Hermit,' he said; he knew it, beyond any question of argument.

8

The summer holidays went by with their usual rapidity. The combine harvesters munched their way through the fields and then there was stubble everywhere and clouds of smoke drifted upon the wind from where it was being fired. Peter tried to keep out of the way of his next door neighbours as much as possible but he could not altogether forget or ignore them.

The two families were now no longer on speaking terms since an exchange of angry letters between the men. Mrs Turner had tried to say 'Good morning' to Mrs Baxter one day as if nothing had happened but had received no reply, and now she managed never to look in Mrs Baxter's direction should they chance to be in their front gardens at the same time. Peter, Janice and Linda all in their various ways tried to pretend as if Peacehaven and its occupants simply did not exist. A remark from Janice to Peter, however, showed that she found this pretended unawareness impossible to keep up.

'Had you noticed,' she said to Peter one morning, 'how Mr and Mrs Baxter are coming out in the garden *together* more than they used? They stand together and look at us. They aren't gardening or anything like that. They were in the front today staring at me as I went out shopping for Mum'.

'Yes – I had noticed, I suppose.'

'They used to be like the little people in one of those old-fashioned boxes that show the weather – you know, when one was out the other was in, and it meant it was going to rain or be fine.'

'I know what you mean,' exclaimed Peter, struck by this analogy. 'And now the weather is – what?'

'The weather is *onimous*,' said Janice, shuddering.

'Ominous, you mean – '

'I know what I mean,' she retorted, annoyed at being corrected.

'I'll tell you another thing,' Janice continued after a moment's muttering of 'ominous' and 'onimous' to herself. 'In their crazy world it's all *our* fault.'

'I don't know what you mean, how could it be?'

'Don't you see? I've been thinking and I know it's silly but everything that's happened has happened from us *first*. What I mean is – first Mum called on *them*. Then she went into *their* garden to get Linda's vest. Then Justin banged on *their* wall, well, it was both our walls I know, but Justin was *doing* it, then, what happened? Oh, then you and David kicked the ball in and wanted to get it back. They must have thought they had to keep us *out*, don't you see?'

'Yes I do see.' Peter, despite himself, was struck by her acuteness.

'I think they're stark, raving bonkers,' she decided as if that ended it.

'They are – and yet they're not. I wish they really were and then men would come and take them away in strait-jackets, wouldn't they? But the trouble is they don't do anything really loony and I bet they never will.'

'I wish they only would!' said Janice wistfully.

Peter found himself often thinking about this little conversation. Certainly it was a new thing, the way the Baxters came out together and seemed always to be looking, or half looking, towards Nut End. And then they began to speak to each other, in half audible voices. One Sunday morning the voices were perfectly distinct and could not be overlooked.

It happened like this.

Peter and his mother were both in the back garden at the same time: he was pulling up a cabbage for her because she did not want to get her fingers all earthy, when they both became aware that the Baxters were not far from the hedge, casting glances towards them.

63

'There they are,' he heard Mrs Baxter say.

'I see them,' came the reply and then, after pausing a moment, he said slowly and clearly:

'We'll get them out of there sooner or later.'

Peter saw his mother's face flush; without a word she took the cabbage from him and went quickly indoors.

He remained a few minutes after she had gone, thinking over what he had heard: it had been only when his mother flushed that the sense of the words had sunk in, and he knew without doubt that the words had been intended for their ears. So the Baxters wanted to try and get them out of their home, did they? How could they possibly do such a thing?

Peter longed to think of some remark he could toss off to himself to show how little such threats could affect him, but in the end all he did was whistle loudly as he returned the spade to its place in the gardening shed. When he looked again towards the Baxters he found they were no longer there.

The morning continued badly. Peter felt sorry for his mother, who was obviously upset, but who would not answer him when he made some little remark about their beastly neighbours. She continued to cut up the cabbage and he could see her hands were shaking. It was early, but he went and laid the table for her in the dining room and then could not think what to do. Janice and Linda were playing some girls' game and did not want him. For what seemed hours he sprawled upon the sofa with the Sunday paper reading all sorts of dull articles he did not really mean to read.

At last Janice and Linda's game ended and they wandered in and out of the room yawning and saying they were hungry.

'Isn't it *ever* going to be dinner time?' he heard Linda call.

He followed the girls into the kitchen.

'Can't we have it without Daddy?' Janice was saying as he went in.

'If he's much later than this we'll have to,' replied her mother rather grimly. 'He said he'd be back by a quarter past and now it's after half past.'

'Where is Daddy?' asked Linda.

'He just popped along to have a drink with one or two of his friends.'

'Oh, you mean he's boozing at the pub,' commented Janice with one of her sharp looks. 'Oh come on, Mum, can't we have ours, I'm starving.'

'But it's a joint and Daddy was going to carve it for me,' said Mrs Turner, looking hot and bothered.

'*I'll* carve,' offered Peter. 'Come on, let me have a try.'

'I'll do nothing of the sort,' returned his mother. 'I'd rather do it myself. I can't think what's keeping him. He really should have the consideration . . . it's all getting so dried up. Oh well, come on children, I'll dish it up and we'd better begin. I expect he'll be back very soon. These men, they're worse than women when they get going . . . jaw, jaw, while their wives are killing themselves getting their dinner ready.'

Mr Turner did not return until they were just starting on their pudding.

At first he was very jolly. 'Sorry I'm a few minutes late,' he said airily as he sat down. 'I was just coming along and then John Steer blew in and so we all had to have another one.'

'Another two or three I should think,' Peter heard his mother mutter to herself. 'Yours is in the oven,' she said out loud. 'Don't blame me if it isn't what it was.'

'Sorry, *sorry*, didn't mean to put you out. If one can't have a drink with one's friends every now and then – '

He fetched his plate and began eating hard to catch the rest of the family up. Peter and Janice kept silent, knowing that both parents were rather more annoyed with each other than appeared on the surface. All might have smoothed over and gone reasonably well had not Linda, who was a finicky, hard-to-please child at meal times, pushed her pudding aside and said in a disagreeable voice:

'I can't eat this now and watch Daddy shovel in beef and Yorkshire pudding like that – it puts me off.'

'Linda, don't be so ridiculous,' snapped her mother. 'I'll not have that good fruit and cream wasted.'

Linda merely stuck out her lower lip and looked obstinate.

'Let *me* deal with this,' said her father firmly, in a loud voice. 'Now Linda, you're to do as your mother tells you. There's far too much disobedience and bad behaviour at meal times. Open your mouth.'

He filled her spoon with fruit and aimed it towards her mouth. Linda turned her head aside and the spoonful spilled over the table.

'Now look what you've done!' she cried.

'You're not to be insolent to me! Eat this up or I'll spank you properly.'

'I don't care,' she gritted through rigid mouth and closed teeth.

'All right, I'll choose a punishment which *will* make you care. Early bed, and no television for the rest of the day.'

'I don't care – ' she was beginning, when a look of anguish slowly spread over her face. 'But it's episode three of *The Little Princess*,' she cried out. 'I've been looking forward to it all week!'

'You can't stop her looking at that, Daddy,' intervened Janice hotly. 'It simply wouldn't be fair!' while Mrs Turner also interjected, 'If she begs your pardon, Jim, can't you let her watch just that, it's a shame to cut her off in the middle of a serial.'

Both Janice and her mother were looking at the now sobbing Linda, who had worked herself into a state in which she was totally incapable of finishing her pudding or of apologizing to anybody, and so they did not see the way in which Mr Turner's face began to redden.

'All right!' he suddenly shouted, making everybody jump, and in his turn pushing his plate aside. 'It seems everybody gangs up against me in this house. Well, if I'm not of any account in it, I'd better leave it, that's all.'

And he strode out of the room, slamming the door.

'Oh dear, oh dear, oh dear.' Mrs Turner sat down, putting her head in her hands. 'If *only* these things wouldn't happen at meal times. That's two platefuls wasted, and I wanted us all to have a good Sunday dinner.'

'It's all right, Mum.' Janice had opened the door to look outside. 'He's only gone down the garden.'

'I didn't suppose he'd gone anywhere else,' replied her mother dispiritedly. 'But – I don't know. I feel like giving up sometimes. I really do. I shouldn't have crossed him like that, I suppose, but I was upset.'

Peter, carrying a pile of plates into the kitchen, saw from the kitchen window his father down the garden digging as if his life depended on it. If the Baxters were in their garden they were nowhere in view.

If they went and made remarks at Dad now they wouldn't half cop it, he thought to himself. One side of him wished that to happen. But he knew it wouldn't. It was the vulnerable and defenceless that were most easily caught by such as they. And then there passed through his mind the thought that his father *had* been going out to the pub more often of late: it was a pity as it did tend to make him rather touchy and irritable on his return. But this had nothing to do with the Baxters – or had it?

'You go and sit down, Mum,' he said to his mother as she came into the kitchen. 'Janice and me'll do all the washing up.' He wanted to do something – anything – to take the hurt look of misery from her face.

'You're a nice boy sometimes,' she said, her face brightening. She walked up to him and gave him a little hug, and Peter felt a pleasantly warm, self-congratulatory glow spreading within. It was the only good moment of that day, however, which continued edgy and bad-tempered, just like the chilly wind which had sprung up outside, bringing clouds over the sun and an end-of-summer feeling already. How could the Baxters get them out? The threat must remain an entirely empty one – surely it must?

9

'And what shall we do now?'

It was the last day of the holidays. For a treat Peter was entertaining his friend David for the day: lunch was over, they had done various things and suddenly there didn't seem anything more. It was inconceivable that David should go home at this early hour – if only they could think of something to *do*.

David restlessly roamed about Peter's garden, seeking entertainment, while Peter for the first time felt a slight criticism of his friend. He wasn't the sort of person you could relax and just fool around with. It was both an honour and a bit of a strain to have the responsibility of him for the whole day.

'Gosh, that barbed wire looks awful,' commented David. It was the third time he had said that. He peered through into Peacehaven's garden. 'Blimey, Linda's ball is still there,' he said suddenly. 'You mean you never got it back?'

'No, we couldn't be bothered,' said Peter in as indifferent a voice as he could manage.

'Come on then, let's nip over and get it now. They'll never know.'

David was referring to the departure of the Baxters on their weekly shopping expedition into the nearest town, witnessed by both boys ten minutes previously.

'Yes, but Mum'll be furious if she sees me over there.'

'She's gone out too,' David reminded him. 'We're all alone, aren't we?'

'Yes, yes we are,' Peter admitted slowly. His mother and the girls had set out just after the Baxters to go down the village and buy various things at the village shop.

'It's jolly stiff wire, but if we put a bit of sack over the top . . .'

'O.K.,' said Peter, not wanting to seem a coward. Anyway it was ridiculously easy and he mightn't get a chance to poke round there with everybody out ever again. His mother and the girls would be a good half-hour at least, and the Baxters would be away about two hours as was their regular habit. It was now or never.

In a minute they were both over the wire and in the garden of Peacehaven.

In a few more seconds Linda's ball, the colours dimmer from exposure to sun and rain over the last few weeks, was sailing back into the garden of Nut End, propelled by David's lusty kick.

Peter meanwhile carelessly sauntered up the path towards the house. This expedition, which would for some reason have been fraught with nervous fear had he been on his own, was totally different now he was with David. He was in the Baxters' garden, and so what? They had changed various things. They had cut down most of the long grass and weeds and there was a good deal of barish earth. The vegetable patch had been enlarged. There was a net over the raspberry bushes with one trapped bird fluttering inside. Peter let it out and sauntered up towards the kitchen. There was no nasty feeling about the garden: why should there be?

David followed Peter up the path to stare in at the back windows of the house. That he was just slightly affected by feelings of tension showed when he let out an exclamation and clutched at Peter. 'Something dark ran between my legs!'

'It's only our cat,' said Peter. 'Here Tap – Tappy . . .' He hesitated in front of David to give the cat her full name: Taptoes, Linda's name for her three years ago when she had been herself only four and the cat a kitten. Now the cat was a self-sufficient, rather small and shy doctored female who had never known the joys and perils of maternity and spent a good deal of her waking life hunting mice and birds. She had been scared by the Baxters' arrival and since then had ventured only into the very bottom part of their garden.

Now, presumably emboldened by the boys' presence, she sat calmly outside the kitchen door washing her face and then looking up at them with a look of inquiry as if to say: 'Well, what next?'

'Their scullery is rather like yours only the other way round,' announced David, peering into it. 'What's that great box doing there, do you see it? Perhaps they have a dead body inside.'

'Where, where?' Peter craned over David's shoulder, shoving David so that his arm knocked into the window. It swung slowly inwards.

'Look at that!' cried David. 'The catch was loose or something. Come *on*, Peter. Now's our chance. Let's get in and look round!'

'That catch always was loose,' Peter commented. 'I once got in that way when old Mrs Joyce had locked herself out, and I was able to undo the back door for her and let her in.'

'So come on Peter, we'll just have a quick nip round shall we? It's as easy as falling off a log. Not scared, are you?'

'Of course I'm not scared,' exclaimed Peter, very aware that he must not seem all wet and cowardly in David's eyes. He might be small for his age, but he was as tough as the next, and so to prove it, without letting himself think any more he had grasped the inside of the window frame, put one foot against the wall, hauled briefly and was up and kneeling on the draining board inside the window, feeling the runnels dig uncomfortably into his knees. Then he jumped lightly to the floor, noticing as he did so that the smell was quite different. The whole house had a distinct smell in Mrs Joyce's time: the clean smell of lavender-scented soap as well as the smell of old lady and old furniture and books.

Now the smell and feel of the house was closer, fuggier, dirtier. The kitchen and scullery, without being noticeably very grimy, had a greasy film of dust over most of the surfaces;

70

the linoleum in the kitchen, a greyish-blue in colour, had the outline of muddy footprints crossing it. There was the imperfectly wiped stain of some dark brown substance which had been spilled near the stove.

'There you are, just like a coffin,' said David as he climbed in, leaving the window wide open behind him.

'No it isn't, don't be silly. It's just a box.'

Peter walked through the kitchen deliberately not letting his mind romanticize this expedition. He was going to look round very quickly – and then out. And he was not going upstairs. Nothing was going to make him go upstairs.

'I don't think they can have unpacked all their stuff yet,' said David, coming to stand beside Peter in the hall. 'There seem such a lot of boxes and packing cases still, don't there.'

'Yes, that's a bit odd.'

Peter opened the door of the Baxters' sitting room and looked in. He was conscious of slight stirrings of surprise here too at the unfinished look of the room, with a big trunk pushed up against one wall. There were no pictures up, no bookcase full of books as his parents had in their sitting room. But the Baxters owned the usual unremarkable kind of three-piece suite that so many people had, this one in a dark greenish material. There was a mustard-coloured carpet upon the floor, a reproduction oak table with four shiny wooden chairs round it and the dark red curtains pulled as usual half across the window, so that the sun came in only slightly, and with a dim, reddish light. There was again a dirty, fusty smell.

'Oh, there's nothing interesting here,' announced David after a few seconds more wandering about. 'Their clock's stopped at one o'clock, do you see?'

'Oh yes.' Peter turned from an anxious survey out of the front window to glance at the clock on the mantelpiece, a big, rather ugly clock of dark mahogany. Three dead flies lay beside it. How long had they been dead? How long had the clock been stopped?

'Let's go. There's not much to see here.'

'Yes, let's.'

They turned back towards the door leading into the hall and it was then that Peter saw the birds.

In the darkest corner of the sitting room, where Mrs Joyce had had a grandfather clock, a large nail had been driven, about two feet from the ceiling. From the nail hung a skein of little birds, tied by the neck one above the other, chaffinches, sparrows, robins.

'Oh golly,' whispered David, advancing and touching one limp wing with his finger. 'I don't like that.'

The skein of birds rotated slowly as he handled it, showing dulled eyes, gaping beaks, bedraggled feathers. A few feathers had drifted down to lie beneath the pathetic corpses.

'Let's get out of here,' exclaimed Peter, who had no desire whatever to touch the birds, to touch anything in this house.

'Yes. Peter – do you think these were ones that – didn't get out from under the netting?'

'Could be.' They both shuddered then and quickly, yet not letting themselves hurry too openly, they walked back into the scullery and swiftly climbed through the open window. When he was safely on the ground outside, Peter found his knees were trembling in the most ridiculous manner. He carefully pulled the window to shut behind him as if it had never been open.

'They'll never know,' said David as they climbed back into the garden of Nut End.

'No, they'll never know,' echoed Peter. He felt as if they'd been away hours, and yet the whole expedition had taken less than five minutes.

'Peter, have you got the cat upstairs with you?'

'No,' he shouted down from the midst of piles of school books, his maths set (or those parts of it he could find), his gymshoes, the bag into which he was supposed to put his gymshoes and football boots . . . Where was his *left* football boot?

72

'Is she shut into any of the bedrooms? Just open the doors and call her, there's a good boy.'

'Blast,' said Peter to himself, concerning the missing left football boot. Nevertheless he got up and opened doors and called 'Taptoes . . . Tappy.'

Silence; no little rushing furry body. Of course the football boot could be downstairs, in some cupboard somewhere.

He clattered down the stairs, to be met by Linda. 'Mummy's going to put Taptoes' dinner to wait outside for her,' she said.

'Oh.' Peter, lost in the approaching world of school, was not very interested. It had gripped him shortly after David had left: the smell of the books, the school clothes, was bad enough. It brought it all back only too vividly: the stench of school, the noise, the pressures of having to be somewhere every moment of the day, the panics over things which he ought to have done and had not done. The feelings of inferiority. The people he didn't like. The people he liked all right but who didn't seem to like him. A few friends . . . David had said he would look out for him on the coach. And of course he had moved up a year. There would be the year's new intake: towards which he, Peter, as an experienced old hand would have a delicious feeling of superiority. Perhaps school had a few compensations after all.

Lost in such thoughts as these, Peter was slow to realize that there was a fuss going on that evening over the cat, who had not returned from her afternoon's hunting to have her supper.

'She's *never* out as late as this,' said Linda tearfully when her bedtime became due. 'I've been all down the garden calling and calling.'

'She was out in the garden earlier on this afternoon,' said Peter, remembering. 'She was with us – I last saw her in the Baxters' garden.'

'Bedtime, Linda,' said her mother. 'She could have gone down towards the farm, you know. She'll be back later on, I expect.'

'She never goes to the farm,' cried Linda. 'She doesn't like their dog. And she's not up the lane.'

73

'Well, we can't search half the village for a grown-up cat who's perfectly able to take care of herself,' said her mother. 'Come on Linda, do, I've run your bath.'

'I'm just going down the garden again,' said Linda stubbornly.

A few minutes later, while the rest of the family was watching television, they were all startled by the door of the sitting room's being flung back against the wall, and then a hysterically sobbing Linda made a dramatic entry.

'I've seen her! I've seen her!' she screamed out.

'Oh for goodness sake stop making such an awful noise, Linda,' said her father, 'and explain properly. What's happened?'

'*Taptoes*. They've got her. I can see her little face pleading at me. They've got her shut up.'

'How do you mean? Whatever do you mean?' exclaimed everybody except Peter, who experienced a sudden dreadful pang of memory. Memory of an open window and of where he had last seen the cat. But she surely couldn't have followed them in without their seeing her? And then he remembered that of course once before, in Mrs Joyce's day, Taptoes had done just that, had jumped in after him, and what was more, she had been rewarded with a saucer of milk by the grateful and appreciative Mrs Joyce, together with cooing remarks along the lines of 'pussy, pussy' and 'what a lovely little cat she is.' Taptoes, where her stomach was concerned, had a good memory: must have thought that the Baxters had gone and wondered if the kind milk-producing lady had miraculously come back again. She had leapt in after them, must then have panicked and run to hide under something, and they had never seen her and had shut her in.

'You mean the Baxters have got Taptoes shut up in their house!' cried Janice. 'We must get them to let her out. Mummy! Daddy! Did you hear me?'

'I'm not going round there and that's flat,' said her father, turning back to the television. 'Anyway, how do you know it's our cat you've seen at their window? They could have got a cat of their own. No, I'm not getting involved in *that*.'

'Yes, Linda, how do you know it's Taptoes?' exclaimed their mother, but she looked uneasy, unsure.

'Of *course* it is, do you think I don't know her dear little face?'

'I'm going out to look,' exclaimed Janice, almost as worked up and upset as Linda while Peter followed them, despair and foreboding gripping at his heart.

And there plain to see was the anguished face of Taptoes at the Baxters' scullery window: worse, she caught sight of them and her mouth opened and shut in soundless plaintive appeal.

'I could get over and push that window . . .' exclaimed Peter. He would have done it too, with everybody about and the prospect of instant apprehension had they not at that moment seen the figure of Mrs Baxter appear dimly behind the cat, looking directly at them.

With one accord and without a word the three of them went back into their house.

Peter turned and turned in his bed that night; harder every moment, it held him in a hot grasp of bedclothes, ground his head into its pillow of concrete and sent his aching brain spinning. But how could he sleep with the knowledge of what he had unwittingly done tormenting him? He did not believe that the Baxters would ever let Taptoes out. He saw her fading away, unfed probably, until she collapsed utterly and they never saw her again . . . They might string her up, by the neck, like the birds.

He and Janice, after talking the whole miserable business over, had finally plucked up courage and gone round to the Baxters' back door and knocked, half hoping that when it was opened the cat would seize her opportunity and run out.

'I can't think how she ever got in,' exclaimed Janice for what seemed the millionth time. 'They never have any windows open.'

'She could have gone in by a door,' Peter had suggested unhappily.

'I think they captured her, just to spite us,' whispered Janice. They had reached the Baxters' back door. Uneasily, feeling exposed, Peter knocked. There was a long pause, then Janice knocked. Still nothing happened.

'They're not going to answer! They *must* answer.'

But they did not, even when Janice went round to the front door and knocked there. Meanwhile Peter, ashamed, but not able to stop himself, walked quickly home.

When Janice too returned she looked utterly stricken. 'I never thought they wouldn't answer,' she said tearfully.

'I *knew* that wouldn't be any good,' Linda called down from her bedroom. 'Poor Taptoes will have to stay all night in that dreadful, dreadful place.'

'Now Linda,' Mr Turner came out into the hall. 'That's quite enough of that. If the cat is still missing by tomorrow evening and you still think you see her next door, I'll go round myself and try and sort it out but I'm not going tonight and that's flat.'

'Suppose they don't open the door to you?' cried Linda.

'Shut up. I'm tired of the whole subject, do you hear me? I've told you what I will do and that's the end of it.'

He went back into the sitting room, shutting the door, tense with the suppressed anger that any mention of the Baxters now aroused in him.

'They won't answer the door to him either,' said Janice, and Peter was inclined to believe her. The powerlessness of their parents to 'do anything about' the Baxters was an added source of bewilderment and worry to them both.

And so Peter, lying in bed and hearing the clock strike eleven and then twelve and then one, became uneasily more and more certain that there was only one possible thing to do now, and that was for him to get up, cross the fence into the Baxters' garden, and under cover of darkness, push their scullery window and let Taptoes out. How pleased she would

76

be, and how simple an operation! He glowed momentarily with pleasure and with pride when this solution occurred to him, and then realized that he had not, in fact, done it yet.

He would do it. Right away. Not giving himself time to think any further Peter got out of bed, pulled on his trousers over his pyjama bottoms, chose a dark jersey for top cover and padded down the creaking stairs, into the kitchen, undid the bolt on the scullery door and was out.

It was a light night, although there was no moon visible. High clouds were passing by rapidly overhead, driven by a warm gusty wind and there was an occasional glimpse of stars. There was a fresh smell of cut grass and of the harvest now almost entirely gathered in from so many of the nearby fields. Slowly Peter went down the garden to the easiest place, crossed the fence (sticking on it for one unpleasant moment and ripping his trousers) and approached the dark bulk of the Peacehaven side of the house. There were no lights anywhere. The blackness near the house and the trembling in his legs made it very difficult to walk at more than a snail's pace. He inched along, his heart pounding, and experiencing such a feeling of dread that when he reached the back wall he had to put out a hand to steady himself or he would have fallen.

The feelings of exposure, nakedness, that he had experienced near Peacehaven in daylight, were nothing compared with what he felt now. It was as if he clung to some cliff face with all the winds of heaven about him and multitides of people staring at him. Why, surely there were people, with flaring torches, shouting to each other not so far away? There was a flicker of a sound, as of distant voices and flame fluttering in a wind. And the house breathing at him like some great beast.

Peter clung to the wall, blinking his eyes. He had been imagining things. There was nothing, nothing but the beating of his heart. His fingers found the window and pushed, and it obediently swung open. He had been fearing that it would not, that the Baxters had discovered this weak spot in their defences and mended it. But they had not. It was black inside the scullery and Peter could see nothing.

There was no cat. He had not imagined that this could be so. He had thought of her as instantly rushing out to him. What to do now? The window gaped before him but he could no more have entered than he could have flown. What if he woke them? Their bedroom was in the front of the house, but even then it was not so very far away. Facing the black cavern of the window Peter had another thought. What if he *couldn't* wake them? What if they were not there to wake? For some reason he found this possibility even more frightening.

'Taptoes,' he whispered. 'Oh, please come, Taptoes. Tap!'

Silence. His whisper died in his throat. As a last resort he mewed gently into the scullery.

'Miaou, miaou . . .'

And then at last a little thunder of scampering feet on bare linoleum, a chirrup, and she was *there*, in his arms. Fumbling to get the window in place, he fled, still holding the cat, over the fence, back back to the blessed sanctuary and comfort of home, where he gave the hungry cat her dinner, and then picked her up again and carried her upstairs to bed with him. For a time she sat on his chest kneading him incessantly with her front paws and purring with a shrill vibrancy he had never heard from her before, then slowly, slowly they both calmed down and slept; the cat now nestled beside Peter who still lay upon his back, his mouth wide open. Outside the wind died and the clock downstairs struck four to be followed distantly by the church clock, a quarter of a mile away.

All was still in the hour before dawn as Peter struggled with his dream. He was walking over fields and partially cleared forest looking for something. At first he was unsure what it was, he searched and searched and then as if one more veil were withdrawn from his mind he knew he searched for a certain man and his wife: a couple who lay long asleep, who should have been awoken. But he could not find the place where they lay: in one year only nettles and brambles had

78

grown up and the forest was returning. Here were the deserted cottages, one or two with the roofs already fallen in. Goats and pigs had trampled in and out and birds nested in the thatch.

But this couple's hut had been a little apart from its neighbours at the edge of the village, and he could find no trace of it nor of the posts which had surrounded it. It had gone in the mists, the shimmering mists which had frightened them all so much.

'I charge you good men and wives, do not forget your duty to these people,' he had cried, the tall man who had once been a knight. 'In ten years' time they are to be awoken. When summer comes round again and the harvest is ripening, search me out and I will end their long rest from which you will all have had such benefit. Remember, I charge you on peril of your immortal souls!' And then he had called to various of the men by name.

Nine years had passed and then in the tenth a plague, the dreaded Black Death, had laid so many so early to their everlasting rest that one youth alone with his eleven-year-old sister were the only ones left from that small village. His parents, his three brothers, the other men the Hermit had mentioned by name with his father as especially charged to awaken the couple, all had sickened and died. The old man, Robert the Hermit, who had been alive ever since the oldest of them could remember, who had so often cheated death and thought to be its master, he too had died, quickly, like dry straw eaten by a devouring flame. The lord and his lady had fled the manor and only a few of their servants remained, and most of the people in the other village, the village some five miles away near the church, they had lived on, and the young man who was also Peter in his dream had with his little sister gone to join them, and live with his father's cousin, a widow, who had space for two more in her little cottage.

What would happen if he could not find the enchanted couple and bring them to life again? It was now the eleventh year of their sleep and the time of their wakening was a year

79

overdue. Might they sleep on for a hundred years, for longer? Was it truly his task, as his father's son and the only man living, to awaken them? He feared that this was so. If he failed in his task, would he indeed forfeit his immortal soul? Father Norbert had told his congregation many times with relish how the bones of the damned crackled and sizzled to all eternity on the hot coals of hell: would this happen to him? True, the Hermit had never spoken of the tortures of hell, but the Hermit was dead, and Father Norbert very much alive. He was only a simple fellow who wanted to enjoy the life which had been spared him: what was to be done? It was not fair, when his heart still ached with the sorrow of losing nearly all his family, when to visit this ghost of a village at all brought the tears gushing from his eyes.

A confused time of trudging to and fro, of worry: a consciousness rather than a vision of the ruined cottages, and far off over the great field where the crops had grown, of the walls of the manor house set apart on its little cleared and moated hill top. The lord and lady had returned and horses grazed in the meadow below the walls: horses for the lords and ladies – oxen and asses for the common folk. The dream changed and ended abruptly as a great pair of yoked oxen with red curls between their ears swung before Peter's eyes, their horns scraped his shoulder, as if the plough would bury him deep in earth.

He awoke, pushing aside bedclothes and a sleepy, indignant cat. It was morning.

10

The great red bull stood in the meadow only a few feet from their back fence. He was in the midst of a group of his wives. Other wives grazed in a strung-out line to the far hedge. There were about twenty of them. The bull, an expression of sentimental amiability upon his face, was slowly licking the ear of the nearest of his womenfolk, who was gazing into the middle distance with a fatuously complacent but also slightly absent-minded look. Peter laughed out loud to see them. The bull looked at him with an air of melancholy reproach through his thick white lashes, and continued licking.

'Peter! Peter!' his mother called down the garden.

'Yes!' he shouted crossly, not wanting to be interrupted. There was always somebody at him to do something every moment of the day: or so it seemed.

'The evenings are really beginning to draw in now.' His mother came down the garden. 'It's getting quite dusky. I don't like the idea of Janice walking down the fields from the church all on her own. So will you go up and fetch her, there's a good boy.'

'Oh, O.K.,' he muttered, not very graciously.

'And hurry yourself a bit, Peter, they'll be stopping ringing soon.'

'I can't hear them now.'

'They often have a break. Or the wind's in the wrong direction.'

'There isn't a wind this evening,' he said, walking back towards the house with her.

'No. I shouldn't be surprised if there wasn't a frost tonight. Off you go then.'

So he set off up the lane, intending to go past Mr North's

bungalow and then turn up the footpath that went up the fields to the church at the top of the hill. It was shorter than keeping to the road. As he passed Mr North's little field he looked out for his friend the goat but she was nowhere to be seen. Somewhere at the back of his mind was the thought that he had not noticed her for some days now. But he had been at school most of the day and there had been this worry which nagged at him.

It was a week ago that he had found it, a piece of paper with the address of a house agent upon it and a list of some fourteen or fifteen houses for sale. The houses were scattered over an area of about ten miles, none in Long Green.

The obvious thing to do would have been for Peter to tackle his mother about this list of houses. 'You're not thinking of moving, are you? I've just found this house agent's list,' or something similar but he found this impossible, perhaps because he was afraid of the answer she might make. So he waited for her to tell him, and she did not; he heard nothing from her or from his father. Neither of the girls seemed aware of this fateful piece of paper, nor did Peter mention it to them. He simply tried to forget it, throwing himself rather noisily into activities at school and failing to do his homework at home. That was the week he got two detentions, never having had a detention before. This would have made him new friends among a rather different crowd of boys had he been interested. But he did not want to make much effort over anybody.

'Anything the matter?' Miss Armitage had said that Saturday as he sat silent in her kitchen.

'I don't know,' he had muttered at first. 'Don't think so. Why?'

'Just didn't think you were your normal chatty self, that's all. But I don't want to pry. Have another jam tart.'

Peter had taken another tart, a rather crumbly one, half of which had dropped to the floor and been instantly cleared up by one of the expectant Sealyhams, and it was while he was picking crumbs off his trousers that he found himself telling Miss Armitage not about the house agent's brochure but about the cause of it, the Baxters.

'Mr Baxter said he was going to get us out,' he found himself saying. 'He said this ages ago, in the summer. And now he comes out into the garden with Mrs Baxter and they talk about us, quite loudly. But we aren't there to hear, if we can help it.'

'How absolutely beastly,' said Miss Armitage sympathetically. 'Can't you make remarks back, or something? After all, there are more of you.'

Peter had not seen it this way. 'We wouldn't be allowed to answer back,' he said at last, realizing the feebleness of what he said. 'Besides, it's the sort of talk which they could always pretend was not about us after all, you know what I mean?'

'I know exactly what you mean. It must be horrible for your mother on her own if they're like that.'

'I don't think she goes down the garden much now,' said Peter, remembering little things, how she always asked him or Janice to get in the washing at the end of the day, how it was his job to dig up or pick for her the vegetables.

'By the way, I meant to ask, what has happened about that wire you told me about dividing the gardens?'

'It's still there. There are letters still going on between solicitors. The Baxters say they bought Peacehaven, when we thought it was only rented. And that they were only enclosing their own property. And Miss Joyce has gone to America for a year and we can't contact her. Nobody seems to know exactly where the boundary lines should be. But I don't really know what's happening exactly because Mum and Dad won't talk about it to us.'

'I expect they're jolly worried about the whole unfortunate business,' said Miss Armitage.

'Yes. Dad's been out a lot lately. I don't know . . .'

Peter's voice trailed off. He could not describe to her the bleakness and unease in his own family and to contrast it the way the Baxters now paraded about the place looking flushed and healthy. It was as if they were feeding on and were nourished by the unhappiness they caused. How could people be like that?

'Mrs Baxter smiles in a different way, too,' he said suddenly. He could not describe it further than this.

'I really am sorry,' said Miss Armitage in a friendly manner, as if she meant it. She lit a cigarette.

'But Peter, these unfortunate things can happen occasionally in a village. It looks as if you've been especially unlucky and got a pair who are more than a little paranoid – that is – not mad, but not exactly normal, but then what *is* normal? There used to be some awfully rum types about the place when I was a girl. There was one farmer who used to lay about him with a stick at the slightest provocation, and he didn't care whom he hit, man, child or beast. We were so sorry for his dogs and horses. Then there were all the peculiar gypsies and tinkers and travelling pedlars calling at the back doors. It's tame nowadays by comparison. Yet even today – well, I've a story or two. There's some who *want* to wilfully misunderstand one, that's my conclusion. Why –' and here Miss Armitage launched into a long, complicated story which she told as if Peter knew something about it already. He could not understand much: except that he remembered his mother saying that Miss Armitage had made some enemies purely through her own obstinacy.

'And so I take my turn arranging flowers in the church and even brass rubbing,' Miss Armitage was saying loudly, her face flushed and her hand with the cigarette in it beating against the side of her chair so that the ash fell over the floor, 'but I haven't been to a church service for, oh I should think it must be fifteen years. I let them all stew in their own juice.'

'Oh yes,' said Peter as politely as he could, but vaguely. Whatever was she on about?

She gave him a glance, and visibly checked herself, getting up and briskly shaking off one of the cats which had entrenched itself upon her lap. 'Down, you silly thing. You can't settle there for the rest of the day, much as you might like to. Yes, as I was saying, village life! Claustrophobic, even nowadays. Little things get magnified. But thank God for the telly, that's what I say. There were far more lifelong feuds before the days of telly. People were bored, and had more time for it. Now anyway most evenings the majority are goggle-eyed round the box. It soothes and calms them, if nothing else.'

'I suppose so,' said Peter, a little lost in these statements.

'How's your sister, Janice, isn't it, getting on with the bellringing?' she bawled at him as he waved her goodbye from the gate.

'Oh, O.K. I think.'

'Well, it's good healthy exercise for a girl, isn't it? Cheerio.'

'Cheerio,' he had said; and now here he was, walking up the cold fields, lit with dim pink light from the afterglow of the setting sun towards the church to fetch Janice back from her bellringing.

'Bim, bam, blang,' echoed at him as he walked up the last field. The newly tiled spire of the church shone brassily; the new clock face gleamed. He went in at the gate past the War Memorial and the grave stones. His grandfather's and grand-mother's headstone was still one of the newish ones. The chrysanthemums his mother had put in a pot at the head of the grave a fortnight ago were dying, the white petals curling brown. Once or twice he had looked up the other Turners scattered around, those he could find. The old ones just disappeared, the graves sank right down, and then he sup-posed they planted other people on top. How many layers of bones would there be in a churchyard? It was an interesting thought. He pushed open the great door of the church and went into the dark musty interior.

Behind the curtain, where the bell ropes hung, four girls and two boys aged from ten to about twelve stood solemnly pulling on the ropes under the direction of old Mr Archer who had been a bellringer himself since the age of ten, having his chance in the First World War when so many men were away. Now several children were learning. Janice and another girl had to stand on boxes to reach the sallies of their ropes, which added to the tenseness of their expressions.

'She won't be a minute,' said Mr Archer on seeing Peter, 'we're just running the bells down now.'

Janice did not give him a glance, so intent was she. So Peter went outside again to wait, standing just outside the church door, looking up at the weathercock flying high amid great peals of clanging sound. The spire appeared to vibrate with the noise. The sky was still stained a brilliant frosty green from which a few red streaks were fast fading. Far off, down the hill where the sharp air smoked in a dusky haze, a small herd of sheep were trotting eagerly after a slowly moving landrover which was pulling a cart of hay. A man stood upright in the cart forking out great bundles of it, and the sheep gathered round each bundle in little groups.

It came to Peter then, watching the sheep, his ears battered with sound, his fingers beginning to ache with the approaching frost, that he could endure anything rather than to leave the village and live somewhere else. The village was part of him; scenes like this were part of him. He had not known that the sight of some sheep running on a cold evening and the church bells jangling could rouse in him such sharp emotion.

'Oh bells,' he prayed, turning back to them because they had power, because since at the age of eight he had refused to go any more to Sunday School he had not been much of a churchgoer, and it embarrassed him to say even to himself 'Oh God'; it didn't seem fair to God in some way . . .

'Oh bells, please make it all right. Please help me. We can't be pushed out of our house, can we? Can we?'

Clang, jam, they exclaimed, and then a single bell, a deep one, the old one, rung by Mr Archer, tolled alone, boom, boom, boom . . .

'Please bells,' he said once out loud, urgently, and then the church door opened and Janice emerged.

'My arms aren't half stiff,' she said.

11

'We're *what*?'

'We're going to look at a house.'

'But why? Why are we going to look at a house?'

'Because it's for sale at a price we can afford and there's a reasonable chance it will suit us, so hurry up and get ready, Janice.'

'But we're not going to move, are we?'

'We might, at that.'

'You never told me!' cried Janice indignantly, but in Peter's opinion nothing like indignantly enough.

'Where on earth is this house?' she grumbled, putting her shoes on. 'Linda, did you hear? We're going to look at a house we might move into.'

'What? What? Where? What?' exclaimed Linda, clutching her Teddy and looking bemused.

'*I* don't know. They never tell me anything.'

'The house is in a quiet cul-de-sac near Uncle Ron's,' said their father, standing at the front door, looking at them with a quietly determined air, as if he were prepared for trouble but was not going to let it affect his actions. 'It was your aunt who told us it was going and the couple were in a hurry to leave so would accept a fair price for a good sale. Come on, Peter, what are you gawping at?'

Peter faced him, beginning to tremble with frustration and a slowly mounting anger. Here it was: what he had been dreading was come. He was not going tamely to accept it as the girls seemed to be doing.

'Why are you thinking of moving?' he asked, in as reasonable a tone of voice as he could manage. 'Why on earth should we move?'

'Because it is getting more and more impossible here and it is making your mother ill,' came his father's answer. Upstairs they could hear their mother moving about getting ready to come with them. Instinctively they all lowered their voices.

'She's not ill! She's not gone to bed,' hissed Linda indignantly.

'You don't have to go to bed for bad nerves and not being able to sleep,' said her father in the same quiet voice. 'No, I'm sorry, children, but we've made up our minds over this. The Baxters are making our lives a perfect misery and it's much better to leave.'

'You'll never be able to sell this house!' burst out Peter. 'People can *think* about moving but they have to wait until somebody buys the house they're in before they get the money for the next one. Why, this happened to somebody's parents at school. They couldn't sell their house at the price they wanted and so in the end they never moved!'

'It could happen to us, yes,' agreed his father reasonably. 'But as it happens I've got a chap at work very interested. He is coming to see it tomorrow.'

'But Daddy, have you told him about the Baxters?' cried Janice.

'Not particularly. But he's a tough kind of chap. I don't think they'll worry him too much. Anyway one doesn't go around telling prospective purchasers every little thing that's wrong with one's property.'

'But – ' Peter's heart began to sink very low indeed. 'You can't surely be *serious* about this, Dad?' he burst out at length. 'We can't leave this village – this house perhaps – but not this village! Why, we've always lived here!'

'The trouble is, finding the right house in the village. The new estate is awfully pricey: we just couldn't get the same for this house and I don't see myself bridging the gap. All the larger houses are far too expensive. The little cottages that have been tarted up are mostly too small. When it comes down to it there are only about three bungalows that would

89

do, and none of them show any signs of coming on the market.'

'We could build a house!' cried Peter wildly.

'Don't be silly. We'd never get planning permission: *and* it would be far too much money anyway. No, we have this opportunity to go into quite a good house, the right size and a price I can afford and I think we should do it.'

'But Dad! Leave the village! What about your friends? Mum,' he turned to her desperately as she came down the stairs, 'what about *your* friends, at the W.I. and the church? And you help out with the infants at the school on Tuesday and Thursday afternoons. What about that?'

'I've thought about all that of course, and so has your father,' she said, with the same resolute air as her husband. 'It will be a wrench leaving everybody, but gracious, Peter, we're not going to the end of the world! It's only six miles. We'll be able to come back and see our friends. And there's a very flourishing W.I. in town. Your father can walk to work and come back for lunch. It will save us no end of money and petrol. We'll be able to afford more trips away, perhaps. There will be advantages as well as disadvantages. Now come on children, if you're coming with us, that is.'

'I bloody well am not!' burst out Peter, now no longer able to contain his impotent rage and misery. 'I don't want to see any rotten town house near our beastly relatives! That awful Justin! You can't let those Baxters win! You're letting them just trample you down.'

'All right Peter, calm down,' said his mother. 'You don't need to swear and shout at us, even if you are upset. If you don't want to come with us, don't. You're old enough to be left alone for an hour or two, for heaven's sake. Linda, you must come with us but Janice, you can please yourself too if you like.'

'Oh, I'm coming,' said Janice immediately.

'Isn't Peter in a temper?' was Linda's tactless parting shot as the three female members of the family went out of the house to wait in the car, leaving Peter and his father glaring at each other.

'You don't understand, Peter,' said Mr Turner slowly after a moment, and obviously making an effort to keep his own temper. 'There's no question of winning or losing in this sort of situation. I've talked it all out with the lawyers and their advice is to leave if it's really getting your mother down, which it is. We have no legal case against the Baxters at all. Surely you don't want her to have a nervous breakdown?'

'No, of course not. But all the same . . . it's all wrong! We must fight the Baxters! They can't *do* this to us! I shall fight if you won't!'

'You're talking wildly, Peter.' Mr Turner's voice was beginning to rise. 'You'll just have to face facts, I'm afraid. I don't want to leave this village myself. But as your mother says, it's not far. We can still see our friends here sometimes. And it's not as though *you* have any particular mates here now, you said so yourself. You'll be not much farther away from this David of yours. You'll be able to bicycle out to him quite easily. And now that's enough argument. Stay at home if you like, and I hope you're in a better temper when we come back.'

'I'm not going! Anywhere! You can't move me out of this house if I don't want to go!' yelled Peter at the closing door. It slammed with a jarring bang in reply and he was left alone in the hall.

'I shall fight! I shan't let you do this to us!' he shouted then, not knowing whether or not his voice would penetrate through the wall. So near and yet so far removed from him were the inhabitants of Peacehaven. He heard his parents' car drive away and a silence descended. He was aware then as never before of a feeling both of smallness and of hugeness: his own body seemed to shrink to insignificance and the unseen Baxters seemed to grow: huge ogre-like figures, they could fill Peacehaven, burst out of it, extend their limbs so that they wrapped round Nut End crushing him within it. Indeed he in

Nut End *was* the nut and he could be broken by monstrous crackers. What could he do?

He drifted into the kitchen, heading for the biscuit tin. He wondered for a moment why it was darker than it should be in there – and then he saw her.

Mrs Baxter stood outside the kitchen window, right against it, so that her nose almost touched the pane. She turned her head slightly at Peter's entry and their eyes met. The expression, or rather lack of expression, upon her face did not change.

Peter panicked. '*She's come to get me out*,' he thought. He could taste the fear as it rose up from his stomach. He turned and ran from the kitchen upstairs to his bedroom where he dived on to the bed and right under the eiderdown, his heart beating at him like some over-driven engine.

Nothing more happened. It was quiet and warm under the eiderdown. Slowly he calmed down and began to rationalize the incident: Mrs Baxter must have knocked at their back door and no one had heard, so she was looking in: what would she think of him for running away? Perhaps she would be knocking at the front door in a minute. But at the thought Peter put his head under the eiderdown again. She might come in; there was nothing to prevent her. None of the doors were locked. She might come upstairs, into his room.

Oh, why had she been looking in like that? How had she got there? Surely she had not climbed over the wire. But had there been time between his family's leaving the house to slip round the side of it from the front, unseen? Unless, unless she had been standing outside the kitchen window for some time, while the Turner family were upstairs, or arguing in the hall? This was not a pleasant idea either.

Time ticked by, and all remained quiet. Peter emerged partially from the eiderdown but remained upon the bed. From his pillow he could see the leafy top of the apple tree begin to lash about under a sudden storm of rain.

They'll have a wet drive, he thought, with sombre satisfaction. Closing his eyes, he listened to the rain until it seemed the only thing in the world; he could not feel his legs or arms, they could be any size, any shape. He could not feel his body.

Totally relaxed at last, Peter let his thoughts drift and pictures began to rise up within his mind, half under his control, half not, while continually hearing the rain.

He saw in his mind's eye his parents and sisters getting into the car and driving off through the rain, and it seemed as if they drove farther and farther away from him not only in distance but in time. The rain swallowed everything, falling ceaselessly, and now other people loomed slowly into his vision, shrouded figures rising through endless thick curtains of mist until he could almost see them clearly: women, their heads covered, some with wisps of long hair escaping and clinging with the damp across their faces, some holding babies and little children tight under their cloaks. Men too he could see; their beards dripping rain and rain running down the long shafts of the spades and mattocks they were carrying. Geese and hens and lurcher-like dogs splashed about in the puddles and round their feet.

These people were all disturbed, angry, and the murmur of their speech could almost be heard above the swelling sound of the rain. There was one woman who caught Peter's attention, a woman bearing a year-old child in her arms. Her face was strangely familiar to him, plucking a far-away chord of emotion from him like a note played gently upon a harp. Then his attention became distracted because the group of people who had been walking this way and that as if uncertain what to do or where to go all stood stock still, and an elderly man pointed and cried out: 'Yes, there he is – Sir Robert – the old Knight,' and Peter saw, coming towards them on a path between some bushes where goats were tethered, a huge man striding, bareheaded, his long white hair plastered to his head with the rain.

'We seek your aid, Sir Robert,' another man cried out, and the old man walked nearer, while the older children and the dogs ran to him and surrounded him and the tethered goats stretched their necks out to him and bleated, and he said gently but in a deep voice of a strangely resonant and penetrating timbre: 'You must not call me Sir Robert, I am plain Robert the Hermit. Nevermore shall I take up my sword against man or beast.'

Robert the Hermit.

The words rang again and again in Peter's ears as they had done once before, and he started up, realizing that he must have slept for some minutes.

The rain was slackening now, he would get up. He would turn on the loudest pop music he could find.

He walked a little unsteadily downstairs, feeling exhausted, almost as if he were recovering from an illness, to be reassured by the quietness and normality of the house. A quick glance into the kitchen showed him that Mrs Baxter had gone: of course she had gone. And then he heard the garage door bang and Linda's voice.

His family had returned, and he was no longer alone.

12

It was nine o'clock of a winter's morning. Peter walked in the wet meadow behind Nut End and Peacehaven, followed at a little distance by the cat. The meadow was for the time being empty of cows. It was white and misty, cold and motionless. It would be Christmas in three weeks. Until then time seemed to be standing still: indeed, in this damp field in which no living thing stirred, it seemed as if nothing could ever happen again.

Nothing was yet definite about the Turner family's proposed move, though this was supposed to be going through within the next couple of months: as far as Peter could understand the matter, no documents had as yet been signed on either side: his parents had not yet actually bought No 12 Oakdale Crescent, as it was called, nor had the man from Mr Turner's office yet bought Nut End, though he had seemed distressingly keen. Peter had gone out each time this man arrived: he could not bear to see him walking round their home and opening cupboard doors and talking about drains. Nor had Peter seen Oakdale Crescent more than once. He had equally hated talk from his mother along the lines of 'Of course the sitting room furniture would look good in here but we'd have to have new curtains,' each word pinning down the likelihood of moving, hemming him in.

'Don't you *mind*?' he said to Janice once, incredulously.

'I don't want to go in some ways, but it would be nice to be near the shops,' she replied in her most perverse, taunting mood. 'It's only you that minds really. You're the odd one out.'

Odd one out! That had hurt him, for some reason. He did not know why but he had pinned a little hope on Janice's support. He ought to have known she would let him down;

just like her. *Shops!* He could have hit her. And he would not speak to her willingly again for days.

'Well, I am what I am and I'm not going to change,' he muttered to himself, jumping the wet tussocks of grass and remembering this conversation.

Indeed, in the last few months he had been more and more aware of himself as a person: a person who he knew was altering all the time on the surface, yet in some inner resilient core of himself remained much the same. Like a rubber ball, perhaps, which one could punch and dent yet which in essence bounced back into shape each time. This awareness made him the more determined to do – what? What could he do? How alter this slow drift to what he felt could only be defeat and calamity for his family? Everything about him, the calm winter weather, the slow drip from the branches and fall of the last leaves, all seemed quietly to accept their fate in a dying world; a world in which any life, any protest would be muffled by the weight of a million sodden leaves, by the motionless weight of the heavy clay beneath them.

But then, out of the apparently empty fields a flock of lapwings rose about twenty yards in front of him and flapped off, slanting sideways in flight so that their white undersides flashed out and then one of them cried out 'Pee-wit, pee-wit' as it flew.

At the same moment a swarm of little birds, finches or sparrows, skittered along the hedge like a swarm of midges, settling down a moment and then all flitting off again.

'I suppose it's you that frightened that lot,' said Peter to Taptoes, who reared a rather frantic face over the tussocks of grass: they had already gone farther from home territory than she liked.

There were several fine trees along the side of the meadow, the dark grey-green of their branches and twigs made a frieze of intricate design against the white sky. Now Peter could see the twigs agitated by rapidly running little bodies as first one and then another squirrel ran from tree to tree, up and down and along to where the twigs mingled, without ever having to descend right to the ground. As he stared after them he became aware that there was someone walking on the far side of the hedge where there was a public footpath.

Suddenly Peter's heart gave a great jump. It was – it couldn't be, but it was like . . .

An elderly man with longish white hair was striding up the path; he had come back to help Peter from so many hundred years ago. But he was walking on . . .

Peter raced across the field, forced his way through the hedge and on to the footpath. Then he pursued the elderly man. He caught up with him and the elderly man turned courteously at his passing and said, 'Good morning.'

Of course he was nothing like, though he was tall and had a fine head of white hair. He was clean-shaven, and the other had had a straggling beard. This man was dressed in a newish modern mackintosh and wellington boots. He was just someone out for an early Sunday morning walk. Yes, and here was his dog. A golden retriever came over to sniff at Peter's trousers. Of course: he might have known. Why should he have thought, for a ridiculous moment, of anything more? Why, they weren't even in the Hermit's territory. That lay over field and lane about five miles to the west.

Yet the Hermit might well have travelled miles about the district. Five miles was little. Would he have visited the church, which lay only a quarter of a mile up the hill?

'I wonder,' said the elderly man as Peter passed him and his dog, 'I wonder if you could kindly direct me to Long Green church?'

'Yes, of course. You go over that stile up there, by the farm, turn left up the lane past some houses, then there's another footpath you can take, or you can go by the road . . .' As Peter directed him he began to feel a little comforted, as if everything were not totally against him. It was a good omen, this life in the fields, this meeting with a tall soldierly-looking elderly man.

And now he had to find the cat, abandoned in the field, or had she already raced for home? She would not have gone into the Baxters' garden, or anywhere near it; indeed, she always now kept to the farther, safe side of Nut End.

He heard her miaowing plaintively just outside the fence at the bottom of Nut End's garden, and walked with her to the gap where they could both get through. 'That's right Tap,' he said to her. 'You follow me. You're all right with me.'

He too kept at a good distance from Peacehaven's garden, and did not once glance in its direction. For the last weeks they had all schooled themselves to ignore Peacehaven, never look at it, and consequently never see if it were looking at them. It was as if the whole of that side of the house had eyes: one could never forget them. Ignoring was not to forget.

'Come on Tappy.' She ran chirruping through the gap, but Peter paused as he followed her. He found various words going on and on in his mind: stuck like a phrase played again and again on a record, and these words were:

'Bring them back to me. Bring them back to me. *Bring them back to me.*'

It was as if he had heard them from somebody within the last few minutes, yet the only speech he had had with anybody had been the elderly man who asked the way to the church. He had said nothing in the least like 'Bring them back to me'; it would not have made sense.

Could he have spoken softly, under his breath, so that it penetrated somehow on a deeper level, into Peter's mind? Messages could be flashed very quickly on a screen which one's conscious mind missed, but which sank deeper into one's subconscious so that one responded without knowing. He had once read a science fiction story making use of this idea. Could the same thing happen through one's ears?

'Bring them back to me.'

And though there was no sense in it, Peter found himself replying as he followed the cat up the garden: 'How? How can I do that?'

13

The week or so of quiet, windless, almost motionless days continued, as if the countryside were awaiting something which never came: a storm, or a fall of snow, or a hard frost. People who early on had said it would be a cold winter were beginning to change their minds. The holidays began, and Peter became more and more conscious that he too was waiting for something: he didn't think it was for Christmas, though Christmas approached swiftly.

'Damn it,' said Mr Turner, also on holiday for a few days and wrestling to put up extra shelves in the garage. 'If I haven't gone and run clean out of nails. And the car's being serviced so I can't drive anywhere and get some more. Tell you what, could you nip over on your bike to Charlie Dawson and ask if we could borrow some? Two- or three-inch nails. We'll need a couple of dozen at least.'

'O.K.,' said Peter; returned with the nails (his father's friend Charlie Dawson had been generous and given a whole tin full), swerved his bicycle somewhere outside Peacehaven to avoid a straying hen from the farm and upset the whole lot into the road.

He picked most of the nails up and replaced them in their tin, and was just reaching for some more which had rolled under the gate of Peacehaven's drive when he was startled by an angry shout.

''Ere you, what are you doing grubbing under my gate? You leave my property alone!'

'I was only – ' began Peter hotly. He had been going to add 'only picking up some nails,' but then paused, thinking and with some reason, that Mr Baxter might think he had deliberately placed them there. So muttering to himself something along the lines of 'Right, you can keep the beastly nails then,' he walked away.

'And if it punctures their car tyres that'll serve them right. I hope they *do* get a puncture,' he thought, not without satisfaction.

He spent the next half-hour or so watching his father work and handing nails to him. As so often on this sort of occasion he was conscious of being a slight disappointment to his father because he could not really work up much interest in carpentry: as for trying to do any himself, no thank you. Carpentry was about the most unpleasant and painful job one could choose to do if one were as hamfisted as Peter knew himself to be.

So he handed nails and stood about, mainly to be companionable; not that they talked much. But after about twenty minutes or so of watching his father work efficiently and happily sawing and planing a piece of wood, a thought struck Peter.

'Dad,' he said, 'Dad, why are you doing this anyway?'

'What do you mean, Pete? I want shelves for all my bits, as I told you. I've been meaning to do this for ages.'

'But Dad, you're just doing it for the next bloke, if we're moving, aren't you?'

Mr Turner stopped abruptly. 'Nothing absolutely definite yet,' he said at last.

'Yes, but it seems sort of a waste of time, doesn't it?'

'No. No. Lots of time yet. It's nice to get sorted out.'

He looked at Peter with a cross, hurt look and turned back to his work, but silently, without the happy little whistle which had been intermittently upon his lips for the last twenty minutes.

And it was then that Peter fully realized how little his father wanted to leave; that he had indeed temporarily forgotten that they *were* proposing to leave, that in some ways he was finding it as difficult to face up to all that leaving entailed as Peter was.

100

Poor Dad, he thought with an intuitive flash, seeing his father for the first time as a man to be pitied; a man, not quite as young and resilient as he had been, trying to do his best for his wife and family: and he realized also for the first time how little real freedom a well-meaning adult might have, given various unfavourable circumstances. He understood all this, and yet he could not help resenting his father for his helplessness.

It's simply not fair, he thought, and though he had both said and thought these words many times on previous occasions, then he had thought them as relating to himself and his concerns; now his imagination was entirely held by his parents' predicament and he began to understand the great difficulty his father must have had in coming to a decision to leave Nut End.

'Peter, Mum says what are you doing, you promised to dig up a cabbage for her.'

Janice walked up behind him, brushing against him, but not looking at him.

'Oh all right,' he grumbled. 'But you needn't push in like that.'

'I didn't push,' she snapped instantly.

And yet she could not leave him alone, hanging about, singing loudly, and carefully not looking at him as he dug the cabbage.

She was in what he called to himself 'one of her silly moods', at a loose end, disagreeable, wanting to expel her disagreeableness on him, just waiting for an opportunity.

He was not going to give her an opportunity. She was in his black books entirely through her own fault: she could stew there. And so in silence he took the cabbage into the kitchen and then went out to the front of the house again.

As he hung about there, he was aware of two things, first that Janice was watching him from the sitting room window, and also, although his back was turned to them, that the Baxters were preparing to go on their weekly shopping expedition; their car was brought out of the garage and he was conscious of them both going to and fro several times between the car and their house. Then he heard the click and scrape as their gate was drawn back and the noise of the car engine being started up. As Mr Baxter reversed the car slowly out through the gate, Peter looked round. He heard a scrunching sound as the car turned on the gravel of the unmade-up road, or was it the sound of a car driving over nails? There certainly had been more than one nail he had been unable to pick up. Then they had turned and were off, driving slowly round the corner.

'Dad, Dad, I'm just going somewhere on my bike for a bit,' Peter called hurriedly, racing to get it. He could not explain why, but he suddenly had an overwhelming urge to follow the Baxters. It was mad, he knew, a bicycle trying to keep up with a car, but, but . . . they *did* drive slowly. He wanted to keep them in sight if he could, he did not know why.

It proved easier to do this than one might have thought. There was an obstruction along the village street; the dustmen loading their lorry had parked at a narrow place: the Baxters had to draw in behind it to wait for another car to drive past and Peter was able nearly to catch them up. Then they slowed at the crossroads, turned right, and for a short time he lost them.

He pedalled hard for a long quarter of a mile down the road, cursing himself for being a fool. He would never catch them now. What did he think he was doing anyway?

At last he reached another crossroads. It just proved how mad he was: there would be no sign of them, nothing to show which way they had taken. There were no cars, no traffic of any sort, the morning rush hour being over, it was a quiet time of day.

But a few yards down one arm of the crossroads he found Miss Armitage, clutching a dog in her arms, others attached to her in a snarl-up of leads, her hair standing up about her head more than ever and her face red with anger.

102

'Do you know what they nearly did!' she called to him. 'Those neighbours of yours in their beastly little car! They almost ran over Bunty! I'm sure it was deliberate. Poor little thing! She was just sniffing at something in the road, quite near the verge, not on the lead, as she's the one of my dogs I can trust to be perfectly sensible with traffic, and that brute of a man, Mr Baxter or Thatcher or whatever he's called, made a dead set at her. Frightened her badly, poor little thing, and she got rolled over in the dust, but I don't think she's hurt.'

Fat Bunty was held towards Peter, panting, rolling her eyes and looking much the same as usual.

'I shouted something really rude after them, I can tell you,' Miss Armitage continued. 'But it's like water off a duck's back with those sort of people. The woman just gave me a slimy grin. I think she was obviously enjoying the whole thing.'

'So they went up this way then?' asked Peter.

'Yes, yes. The man's an atrocious driver. Slap in the middle of the road.'

Peter swung his leg over his bicycle saddle and pushed off hurriedly.

'I have every sympathy for your mother for wanting to move,' Miss Armitage called after him as he went, and he smiled back at her and waved his hand, though inside himself he had been for some time a little disappointed and angry with Miss Armitage.

When, some weeks ago, he had told her his family were going to move she had been sympathetic; she had expressed sorrow at the thought that she would eventually lose her car cleaner, but she had not expressed the horror she should have felt and she had changed the subject too quickly altogether. It had been then that Peter realized that he had been half hoping she might be able to help them, know of another house they could move into in the village, something like that. Of course she had not; it had been silly of him to hope for anything, he knew it, and yet he could not feel towards her in quite the same way again.

While these thoughts continued in his mind, his legs bore him on and on, round corners, and he found himself set upon a meandering course up a hill towards a little wood at the top. He knew this road, but not well. It was certainly not the quickest way into town: it was not a way to anywhere particular. Where did the Baxters think they were going? Had they been led astray simply by the chance of running over a dog?

At the top of the hill, where a narrow lane intersected the slightly more major road he was on, Peter stopped again. He was now in a very quiet and rural part of the country with many little fields and interconnecting lanes. It was confusing, easy to lose one's sense of direction. But there was a signpost pointing down the narrow lane which said 'Fairfield Green 2 miles' and from the direction of the lane he thought he could hear the receding noise of a car.

And so Peter took a chance and took the turning down the lane, as he did so wondering again what he was doing: was he crazy?

And yet he knew he had to go on, especially as he must be drawing near the part of the countryside in which everything had begun. He was approaching Fairfield Green by a different route from the road which he and Janice had returned by in the summer. On one side of the lane patches of scrub and woodland now began to appear and a rutted track curved off into the woodland. It had a familiar look: did he approach a piece of country he had once partially explored, only from another direction? Here was yet another signpost. 'Fairfield Green, bridle path, ½ mile.' A short cut, evidently. The lane led on half round a corner – and here Peter found them.

The Morris lay canted over very much on one side, with not one, but two flat tyres. It was obviously completely undrivable. A number of cardboard boxes piled in the back had fallen one over the other and Mrs Baxter still sat in the front, but at an angle. She had obviously been too inert to bother to get out. Mr Baxter stood by the car ruefully inspecting the damage.

Peter would have been sorry for them, had they been

104

anybody else. As it was he descended from his bicycle and stood, his breath rasping painfully in his throat.

Mr Baxter looked up and grunted. 'Oh, it's you – you'd better get off to the nearest garage and tell them we're stuck here.'

No word like 'please', Peter thought. But at least Mr Baxter had not connected his punctures with the spilled nails; indeed of course he had never known that the nails had been spilled.

'I don't know where – ' Peter was beginning slowly when he became aware of footsteps coming along the lane behind him. He turned to glance back round the corner and was just in time to catch sight of a tall upright figure and a white head disappearing down the bridle path into the woods.

He knew nothing then but of the importance of following that – person, whoever he had been. And he knew also, though he had no explanation for it, that he must persuade the Baxters to abandon their car and go with him.

'There's a short cut to Fairfield Green just a few yards back,' he said rapidly. 'There might be someone who can help you there. I think there's a garage somewhere about. But you must come with me.'

'Why?' said Mr Baxter instantly and suspiciously. 'Why can't you take a message for us?'

'Because – because – ' began Peter almost in despair. He felt utterly caught in a trap: his reasons for making the Baxters follow him were beyond any kind of rationality, and yet he was being countered by rational argument in the everyday setting of a winter's noon and punctured tyres. It was entirely natural that Mr Baxter, being the sort of man he was, would not want to walk far from his car, and that his wife should still continue sitting, an immovable lump, within the car.

However, the problem of Mrs Baxter's inertia was unexpectedly solved for Peter by Mr Baxter himself, who kicked irritably at one of the good tyres and then called out to his wife: 'What do you think you're doing, staying in there? Do you think a great lummox like you is doing any good to these tyre rims then?'

'Oh, all right, all right,' she grumbled, beginning slowly to heave herself out. 'Don't know what you thought you was doing driving down this lonely place to begin with. Why didn't you go the way we usually go?'

'I wanted to explore a bit, like what I said,' he shouted at her.

'Oh no you didn't.' She straightened up to stand beside him. 'You wanted to give that old woman and her dogs a scare, that's what. I know you. Now look where you've got us to.'

'Oh shut up.'

'Please, you must follow me, both of you, to the garage,' interjected Peter desperately, but they did not move.

He did not know how long he stood confronting them and not knowing what to do; probably it was not more than a few seconds, and then a dog padded into view down the lane, a dog of the cheery, hound-like mongrel type who was obviously out for a walk by himself, seeking entertainment of some kind.

This dog approached, grinning and waving his plumy tail. And then suddenly he paused, his eyes fixed on Mr Baxter. He growled and broke all at once into a sharp salvo of barks. Then he began retreating slowly backwards, his eyes still upon Mr Baxter's face. Finally he turned tail and scurried back along the way he had come.

This most uncanny reaction on the part of the dog sent a cold trickle of fear down Peter's spine, but it also strengthened his resolution. Somehow he must break down the compelling barriers of normality and force them to follow him, if he could not persuade them. He had thought himself tough; here was an opportunity to prove it. Now was the time when the imaginative and the active sides of his nature must finally join together. He did not know from where he found the strength for his next action, but throwing aside his bicycle with a sudden resolution, he forced himself to one act of desperate courage. He ran up to Mrs Baxter, worse, he touched her, he snatched her handbag from her cold flaccid fingers and he ran with it, his head held low as if he were a Rugby forward with the ball, back and along the bridle path towards the unkempt beginnings of the wood. Somewhere ahead of him through the leafless trees he saw a gleam of white hair; he knew he must follow, to where the power of the Hermit lay most strongly, and it gave him courage to cry out: 'You are to follow me, both of you, in the name of Robert the Hermit. Remember the Hermit!'

He glanced once behind him. Yes, they were coming, stumbling and lurching along the rough track, Mrs Baxter's mouth open and her hat askew. There was a chattering commotion all about them, jays flew shrieking through the trees; little birds twittered and whirred their wings: the noise was all birds.

The Baxters were being mobbed. Now there were three or four crows scolding and swooping down at them. There was a tangle of lesser birds, sparrows mostly, also chirping and fluttering about their heads. It was like the owl Peter had once seen in broad daylight pursued by a host of little birds. It was like the fox he had seen trotting calmly over the field with a dead something in his mouth being shouted at and divebombed by magpies and crows. 'Wrong! Wrong! Bad! You shouldn't be about now!' That's what all the birds had been clamouring. This was happening to the Baxters, yet it did not stop them following on and on after him.

And now it felt more and more as if he were being pursued by something both evil and uncanny and he began to be very afraid. He cast the handbag aside because he could not bear the touch of it any longer and began to run again. And as he ran the white mist began to close about him and somewhere ahead he saw a tall bearded elderly man of whom he was afraid yet whom he also had once loved and trusted and he shouted to him, the words coming to his lips without thought:

107

'I return them to you, good Sir Robert, they were at their old tricks, please may they sleep again?' and he saw the old man raise his hands and say something. And then, looking back over his shoulder again he saw to his relief and horror the Baxters begin to fall apart, as if the stuffing were coming out of them. Her hat came off, and she began to stagger as if she were drunk. He fell to his knees mouthing something inaudible and began to crawl, but limply, ineffectually along the path. Then she rolled over on to her back, her mouth open and he came to rest beside her, his nose in the dust. They wriggled a little and were still.

Peter turned away, his own knees weakening and dissolving. Huge drifts of sleep came over him. He felt himself dropping into a sea of cotton wool, but as he fell he knew he cried out desperately:

'But not me! I want to wake up again! I must wake again!'

A great white silence swallowed everything up.

14

Layers of time lapped him round: he was wrapped deep, sunken into the weight of year upon year upon year: deep pressed like the earth with the ever-accumulating debris of more than six hundred years. Yet within this distance and depth he found he watched a scene being played out; it began distantly as a dream but soon he realized how closely akin he was to one of the actors, and then he was within the scene, playing it himself, feeling the emotion, shivering in the cold, smelling the mud and the wood smoke.

It had been a miserable evening, a miserable day. Rain and cold winds had snatched at and beaten the half-grown crops to the ground. It had been like this on and off for many days. First of all they had had a bad spring with frost nipping off most of the fruit blossom and withering the first vegetables, and now what sort of harvest would it be? The village people were cold, ill fed and miserable; and now an additional calamity had occurred: sometime the previous night nearly all their small herd of pigs had disappeared, and though all day youths and boys had searched the thickets and visited all their favourite wallows nobody could find a trace of them. It was just possible their disappearance was due to some marauding band of robbers: times were bad, and thieves and vagabonds were known to hide out in the forest, plundering pilgrims on the road and even raiding the fields of honest folk. Perhaps someone had tipped the robbers off and would secretly share in their ill-gotten gains?

There was a couple in this village capable of doing just that. They never shared anything; always demanded more than their due; squabbled endlessly with men, women and children alike; and so when someone found Wat the Thatcher's wife chewing what looked like a fresh piece of pork (only she gulped and stuffed it down too hastily for them to be sure) the feelings of the village had boiled right over and in spite of the rain more and more of them joined the group of women who had first made the discovery.

'Come on, where is the rest of the meat?' shrieked one of the women, rain dripping down her back as she bent to peer in at their window. A piece of hide hung across the gap and obstructed her view so that she could see nothing.

'I know what it was you were sucking, my *good* dame Betty.' This last was shrieked with evident sarcastic intent.

Another woman plucked at the mantle of the first. 'Oh leave her, it's useless.'

'Useless! It's useless to let them get away with any more. Give us a little suck too, good dame. So kind with your favours. Perhaps I can suck at your breast too – if the rancid thing doesn't choke me!'

'Oh, leave her. Surely they are among the damned, if they cheat us so. They will get their punishment later.'

'Later! What good is that? How do we *know* that what Father Norbert says about the damned will happen to them? Priests can tell their tales, but what good does it ever do to poor folk here and now?'

'Oh hush, Margaret,' the other woman cried. But the first, a big, buxom woman, no longer very young and with all the conviction of the years behind her, cried out again passionately.

'The woman skulking in there has more to answer for. What about that time last year when my own daughter, only sixteen, lay in childbirth before her time and everybody was at a distance in the fields except this woman and she stirred neither hand nor foot to help and the baby, my first grandchild, was born dead! What about that?'

'The child would have been born dead anyway,' said one of the men, coming up behind her. 'As you said, it was strangled by its own cord before it ever drew breath.'

110

'Yes, but she got no help, no comfort, the poor girl,' and the buxom woman began to sob and turned away from the window.

The men behind her were obviously sympathetic, but shook their heads at the women. 'These things must be proven,' said one. 'If anybody has caused a child to die, or stolen a pig, let them come to trial, that's the way.'

'Trials take too long,' shouted a tall thin man, who stood a little behind the others. 'You have only to look at his face now to tell how guilty he is. How about the old way: how about ducking the pair of them in the pond? What about a good beating? If they die under it, it proves they were guilty!'

The lowering figure of Wat the Thatcher, who was also the image of a man named Baxter, stood at his cottage entrance.

'Gerroff, you dirty ignorant knaves!' he shouted, squaring his fists, his face purple with anger.

Now all the men began to shout among themselves, and a long wrangle about the missing pigs began and it became clearer and clearer that nothing could ever be proven, however reasonable or unreasonable their suspicion.

Still the rain poured down, yet the people did not want to go to their homes. They stood in groups talking together, sheltering under the eaves of their cottages and under the trees. They were so wet already that more water made no difference. Indeed, they had the look of people whose desperation was, for the time being, worse than their misery, although many of them stood barefoot in the rain and others had only rough wooden clogs to protect their feet. Tunics and hoods were splashed with mud and ragged with age. One or two of the younger women were better dressed in long warm dresses and cloaks; their hair neatly braided, but they too were soaked and bedraggled, their faces pinched and white.

The tousle-headed children looked happiest, splashing with the dogs through the mud as though it were their natural element.

'The reeve told us, Walt and me, that the lord still claims

every part of our work,' said one gaunt, pock-marked man. 'Although *his* fields have not suffered. He must raise money because he's off fighting again – '

'Who with this time?'

'Don't come to me for an answer. The doings of these mad barons are not our business.'

'Why do you say that? If they ask us for food and men-at-arms they *are* our business – very much so.'

'All barons are not like our baron,' put in a woman at this point. This was a young woman with long fair plaits holding a solemn-eyed little girl by the hand. 'I met pilgrims upon the forest road a month back: among them a couple, man and wife, who spoke of their kind lord and the goodness and generosity of his lady. Every Sunday they feed up to twenty poor people at his gate: nobody is ever turned away, the good wife said.'

'But *we* don't have a kind lord,' said somebody bitterly.

'*Or* a fair-dealing reeve or good luck or even good weather!' complained another voice.

'And we have *them*, those poisonous cheating toads! Was ever a village so unlucky?'

'We are not so unlucky as all that. We also have Robert the Hermit.'

A boy's voice rang out suddenly, in the hush of the slackening rain: the boy was a boy called John; tall, fairer than Peter, but he resembled Peter: indeed he was Peter. Peter recognized him and remembered, and melted into him as two drops of rain on a pane of glass roll together and become one. He felt the wet tunic clinging to his shoulders, the mud between his bare toes, and the embarrassment of having everybody look at him so that his gaze became directed to those self-same toes.

There was a silence for a few moments and they all heard the wind sighing in the trees and the cawing of a few far-off crows and then an elderly man said, 'The boy's right. Perhaps Sir Robert can help us. Father Norbert is useless enough; he only tells us to pray for better times. But Robert the Hermit can heal animals and men – and more than that.'

'But where *is* Robert the Hermit?' spoke up a woman who had kept silent up to now; a woman with a year-old child under her cloak, and she looked at the boy John and smiled, and Peter recognized her and knew that she had been his mother. And then he saw and recognized the three little boys who were his younger brothers running this way and that between everybody's legs.

'That's true,' said somebody. 'Sometimes he is not seen for months at a time. He's not often to be found at his shelter in the woods.'

'Has anybody seen him since Easter?'

'Oh yes,' said an old man. 'He was with my wife last month as she lay dying. He helped her to go easily.'

'I've seen him since then, only the day before yesterday,' cried the boy John. 'I was looking for birds' eggs and he passed beneath the tree in which I was sitting. He was talking out loud to himself but I didn't hear what he said.'

'Sir Robert the Hermit is a very wise man; he knows much of the world, of things both natural and unnatural. He might indeed have been talking with the saints,' said the old man whose wife had died, in rather a snubbing tone of voice.

'Or with the spirits of the forest,' said a woman softly. At her words a little shiver ran through the crowd and it was then that the old man cried out, 'Yes, there he is, Sir Robert, the old knight,' and the huge man appeared, striding through the trees. He was head and shoulders bigger than anybody there and could have been formidable, but when he had reproached them for calling him 'Sir Robert', at which they all grinned in an abashed way because they knew they were continuing to call him by his title out of the great respect they bore him, he sat on a pile of logs in their midst and first the solemn-eyed little girl ran to him, then John's three little brothers, and then all the other children clustered about him, and the dogs approached, lay on their backs and licked his hands.

113

'I've nothing to give you, stupid fellows,' he said to them gently and then looked up, noticing the wild, urgent look of the crowd, and said in a different voice, 'but what is the matter?'

A clamour of voices instantly arose: 'Our pigs? Where are they?'

'Our lord works us to death!'

'We will have no grain this summer and no hay for our beasts.'

'The rain never ceases.'

'The rain *has* ceased,' said the Hermit, holding up his hand. 'You have been babbling like the brook and thought it the sound of rain this long time.'

'Indeed it has stopped,' murmured the woman who was John's mother. She unclasped the baby's arms from her neck and handed her to John. 'Hold her a moment and I will get a torch. It is not right he should strain his eyes in the dusk – '

She disappeared into a cottage and came back with a flaming piece of wood. It served to show them how dim indeed the light was growing.

'But there are two in this village who are not here,' said the Hermit, after he had been brought some milk and a little oatcake which was all he would accept from them. 'Are they ill in their hut?'

'Not ill, Sir Robert, but bad.'

'Do you think they could be witches, Sir Robert?'

'Father Norbert says he can do nothing with them, that they will get their punishment hereafter if they will not acknowledge their sins, but in the meantime what are we to do? *We* are punished daily by having their festering malice always with us.'

'In what way can I help this, friends? How can I cure original sin: sin which is in you and in me also? Indeed I have done enough damage in the world in my time. Which is why I gave up the profession of arms, as you know.'

'You see, Sir Robert – I mean master – it's like this,' a fair, slow-speaking, honest-looking man began, and Peter knew him with a thrill of pride and pleasure for his father.

'Speak out, Will. Speak for them all, for you always speak with reason.'

'It's like this,' said the man who had been Peter's father. 'You see, times are hard. Indeed they are getting harder. I was only a lad when the old lord was alive, but as you know, his rule was easier upon us. We all remember better times, and it's bitter to go downhill, so to speak. But that we might put up with, and the weather, which can't always be as we would wish, had we not this couple, Wat the Thatcher and his wife, who continually plague us.

'As you remember, before Easter many of us were sick with a shaking fever but this woman thrived, nor would she join with the few women who remained well seeking out herbs in the forest for those who suffered. Two babies and four old people died then, and those that were very ill and lived might not have done so had you not then visited us in the nick of time, Sir Robert. Are they witches, and should we punish them for that? Is this why they thrive while we sicken? I would say they were possessed by devils, but if they are, the devils do them no harm. I had heard that those who had a devil screamed and writhed upon the ground? Indeed this is what happened to old Jake the swineherd five years back, and you came and drove the devils out of him. He became much quieter and died a year later, saying his prayers. So it seems as though there is not much we can do about Wat, who is perhaps not a witch and has no devil, and yet we are all so roused up against them that there could be murder done, master, and that's what scares me. See, you get originary folk driven to the end of their tether – and then – what can we *do*, sir?'

'It is time I went and talked to Wat the Thatcher and his wife,' said the Hermit, getting to his feet and grasping his staff.

And it was then that something rather frightening happened.

As the Hermit was slowly rising to his full height there was a long mutter of thunder in the distance and at the same time the

Hermit staggered and dropped his staff. He rocked from side to side on his feet, staring up at the sky, and suddenly startled them all by shouting out in a loud voice: 'Death! I see Death ahead of us! He smites and he slays and the people crumble before him and turn black! I see women dead, their babes at their breasts, I see strong men sicken and die, I see the cows lowing unmilked in the fields! I see the ungathered grain fall to the wild beasts and birds! I see bodies as many as the leaves that fall from the trees thrown together in great pits! Oh God's children, repent your sins for this dreadful time is surely coming.'

Having shouted this out in a great voice the Hermit appeared a little confused. He passed his hand over his face once or twice, bent for his staff, and smiled at the crowd, which had fallen back from him a pace or two in disarray.

'Well, good folks, where is the hut of Wat the Thatcher?'

It was as if he didn't quite know what had happened.

'What is this Death he speaks of?' whispered a young woman to a wrinkled elderly woman who stood beside her.

'I don't know, but it is a Death the Hermit has been prophesying for the last twenty years and it hasn't come yet. Perhaps it never will,' murmured the old woman comfortingly. 'For my part, I'm a going to die peacefully of old age, in my bed.'

'That's Wat's hut there,' people were beginning to point and shout. 'Come out Wat and show yourself.'

Wat stood alone upon the threshold of his cottage, his arms folded over his chest.

'We would like your wife to come out and stand beside you,' said the Hermit gently and with courtesy.

'She's afeard, you see, of those shrieking cats of women. She won't come out, not she.'

'Perhaps one or two of these good wives could persuade her if they went within,' said the Hermit, a little smile upon his lips.

'Nah. I won't have that. Woman! Come out and stop

skulking in there.' He disappeared briefly and came out dragging his wife by the hair.

'Here she is. You can have her for all the good she is to me,' and he spat in the general direction of the crowd, while his wife wiped her nose with the back of her hand and smiled ingratiatingly around, though without quite meeting any-body's eye.

'You know how the people are roused against you both, have you anything to say to that?'

'Yes, I've plenty to say! Unjust, every word of it! Why, it's they that persecute *us*, won't leave us alone for a minute. Only the other day Will there sent his cur into our hut while our backs were turned and he stole a cheese, a large piece of cheese, and took it back for Will and his boys to feast on. Specially trained the animal was, by my reckoning.'

'You know very well I whipped my dog and sent you another cheese, a whole one, by the hand of my son John,' retorted Will.

'Yes, I gave it you, and your wife was by and she saw me,' shouted the boy John hotly.

'We never had no cheese,' said the couple together, with closed, hard faces. 'And there's another thing while we're talking of food,' and Wat the Thatcher began a long shouted tirade in which he involved more and more of the crowd, so that once more there were fists and sticks raised and tempers rose near to boiling point.

'Silence!' shouted the Hermit at last.

But Wat the Thatcher was so purple with anger that for a time he could not be stilled, shouting buck rudely to the Hermit, 'Oh shut your gob, old man.'

'If you can't speak more respectfully to your betters I'll slit your tongue for you!' shrieked a woman, and for a moment it seemed as if the hubbub would only grow worse, but the Hermit waited, still as a stone, his hands clasped upon his staff until at last there was quiet.

'At first I thought that perhaps you were a couple not far

117

removed from the beasts, who pursue their own course and don't care or know whether it harms others or not; had you been like this you would have needed charity and patience and not punishment, but I see this is not the case. It is written over both your faces that you know very well what you are about. I see no great devils there; no major source of evil, but endless petty malice, selfishness and anger. And your anger spreads; it is catching. Will is right: there could be murder done. I believe there is only one solution for people of your kind. I must send you back into the earth.'

Wat the Thatcher paled visibly and his wife ran up to the Hermit and grovelled in the mud before him. 'What do you mean, master?' she cried hoarsely.

'I mean not your death but that everybody must have a rest from you and you must sleep awhile, say for the length of ten years. When you are awoken there will have been time for all these petty ills to have been forgotten on both sides and perhaps you can start again. And if you are not cured you can take my oath on it you will be returned to sleep again, for another ten years, for a hundred, for a thousand perhaps. Who knows? The gods in the forest have their own time. Do not shrink from me when I speak of the forest gods. Father Norbert has forbidden ordinary Christian folk ever visiting the old shrines, and he has reason. But I have now lived long enough and learnt enough to know that there are many different spirits about this earth: to each its own time and season. Doesn't the water mill need the power of the water? And the windmill a wind, from whichever direction it blows? And all souls a cure? I can do it, with the right help. Don't I call myself a healer? Let him who knows other come to me and tell me . . .'

While the Hermit was speaking and arguing with himself it had grown very dark and quiet. Torches cast long, jagged shadows. The very little children had long disappeared from the scene, and their mothers who had laid them to rest were now stealing back into the crowd, anxious not to miss anything.

118

A nightingale began to call from deep in the woods, content that the rain was over, having no part in human suffering.

Wat the Thatcher and his wife stood together, looking about them defiantly.

'Yah, I don't believe he can do it!' Wat suddenly shouted. 'I'm not feeling sleepy yet, and when I *do* choose to sleep, I shall wake up tomorrow, same as always.'

'Make a large fire, here,' the Hermit ordered. He strode about, assisting the putting on of logs. He appeared excited, indeed more elated than anybody had ever seen him.

'If I do wrong in calling up this old, strong magic, I am truly repentant,' John heard him say to himself more than once, 'but I do it to save some poor fellow a greater sin. Creatures of the earth must be returned to the earth, malice as old as time needs to rest. Does not the harshness of winter give way to spring every year? Does not the north wind slacken and die?'

Soon the fire was lit and began crackling up strongly. The Hermit ordered everybody to sit upon the ground and not to move.

'Now I want some men to drive in a few posts around Wat's cottage – just to mark out the place, because after the great sleep comes down you must not go within those posts until it is time for their awakening. If a child strays within a moment he will come to no harm, but it's not good to have people trampling to and fro. The cottage will disappear, you see . . .'

The Hermit smiled and nodded benignly but a thrill of unease went through the villagers seated upon the ground. Wat and his wife stood bolt upright, still as statues, before their door.

Now the Hermit began to pace slowly round the fire talking to himself in a sing-song voice, mostly in snatches of rhyme and poetry:

'Ten long years of sleep,
　　Bed them soft and deep,
Cover them with the sky,
　　Drain their deadly malice dry.'

119

The flickering light made him seem taller than ever and he lost the everyday approachability and humility which made them all love him and they saw his other side; a knight trained in arms who had been formidable in battle, who was subject to powers which perhaps he himself only half understood. He paced about the fire, crying out and laughing and lunging with his staff and slowly, slowly, a great white cloud of smoke arose from the fire and began coiling about the village, between the closely placed cottages.

Somebody cried out in fear: 'Look at the mist coming from the woods,' and they all screamed and began scrambling to their feet as a luminous wall of white, shining out in the dark, began to roll in from the forest to meet and mingle with the smoke.

'To your cottages every one of you!' called out the Hermit in a ringing voice which seemed to echo strangely about them. 'It obeys me! Hah! It obeys me!' And as they began to run he called after them: 'I charge you, good men and wives, do not forget your duty to these people. In ten years' time when the harvest is ripening they are to be woken . . . Search me out; you must find me wherever I might be . . . Will – Matthew – Walter – you men in sturdy middle life, I charge you and yours sons especially with this task, on peril of your immortal souls. They must wake – their sleep cannot be for ever!'

John heard no more because by this time in panic he was running with the rest of them. The last he saw, before he was dragged inside the cottage by his father, was that the mists had completely engulfed both Robert the Hermit and the Thatcher's cottage, though he could still hear voices, more than one, shouting and screaming.

Then everybody went to sleep wherever they happened to fall. In the morning the Thatcher's cottage was not there. Within the space marked out by the posts was bare earth, which was swiftly to fill with grass and weeds. But the posts remained and no man, woman or child ventured within.

And then, years later, came the evening when Margaret,

120

wife of Thomas the ploughman, walked back from a village seven miles away where she had been visiting her sister with terrible news: many people in that village, she said, were dying or already dead from a plague of which there had already been dreadful rumours upon the forest roads. The next morning Thomas stumbled out of his cottage sobbing, for Margaret herself lay dying: first she had had pains in her limbs and a fever and then a hard painful lump the size of an apple had appeared in her armpit; she raved for water, black splotches appeared down her arms; she frothed at the mouth and knew nobody. And as Thomas was telling this to a number of frightened people he cried out, staggered, and fell to the ground, insensible!

Then the people shut themselves in their huts, but it was too late, the dreaded plague raged among them: the Hermit was found stretched out and cold upon a pathway in the woods as if he had tried to crawl towards the village for comfort; the corpses lay unburied for days, just as he had prophesied, and only two out of the whole village escaped.

John's anguished memories began to lessen, to recede, and again Peter became conscious of the dark weight of the years: he felt rather than saw multitudes of people thronging past and a great wind blowing: gradually the wind ceased and the darkness lifted.

He found that he stood within the woods looking along a wide green path down which he saw a man and a huge white horse pacing towards him. The man's long white hair fluttered about his head, not unlike the white, curling mane of the horse. He walked with one arm about the horse's neck and the horse's large, liquid eyes looked at Peter with such an intelligence within them that he knew it could be no ordinary animal.

The man was Robert the Hermit, but he had subtly altered in appearance; he seemed younger, stronger, more upright, and whatever there had been in him that was a little uncoordinated, a little wild and vague, had disappeared, and a face of settled calm and wisdom smiled down at Peter.

'Give me your hand,' the Hermit demanded and Peter to his surprise found it being shaken heartily. 'Thank you, thank you my boy,' the Hermit was saying, his eyes shining, 'Thank you both for waking them up and for bringing them back to me. Now I am released! It's been a long time: I was over-eager and went away too far when I was first taken from my body, and missed my first chance. But I had to come back; I was bound to them. It was a long, long wait until the great wheels spun round and the planets circled in their courses and you were born and grew old enough and walked out one day by yourself . . . It was not chance that drew you to the place where they lay, you have me to thank for that. Forgive me for guiding your steps, for using you, for sending pictures into your mind. Forgive me also for thinking once that I could play God and try to alter what was to be written. But I have seen my side of the spell to its end, and now I am free. I can roam the broad pastures of eternity. I can go!'

So saying, the Hermit leapt lightly upon the horse's back and nudged it with his heels. The horse flung up its head and whinnied, then turned and began to canter back up the way it had come, between the trees.

'But Sir Robert, please,' shouted Peter after them. 'Please tell me, the Baxters – will they wake again?'

The wind had started up once more, making the leaves surge and whisper all about him and so it was difficult to hear Sir Robert's answer as he halted the horse for a brief moment halfway up the green ride and turned to look towards Peter. Was it 'Not in your lifetime'? Was it 'Not for a lifetime'? Was it perhaps 'Not another lifetime'?

And then Sir Robert raised his arm and cried for the last time: 'Go to sleep.'

As he and the horse finally disappeared from Peter's view, the leaves were beginning to be torn from the trees by the great wind which had arisen again; at first mostly green leaves fell, but then there were all colours: red, yellow, white, brown, they whirled all about him making it impossible for him to see anything but them. Did they make patterns? If he could only watch them long enough surely their swirling shapes and colours would form into something of great significance to him; would give him a sign to follow for the rest of his days. Where he looked close at hand there seemed a wholly random blowing and drifting, but deeper near the heart of it all, surely, a kind of form, a relationship of one leaf to another and so to a whole was growing . . .

The colours of the leaves were so bright, beating about his eyes, that he felt he must open them and as he felt this he realized that they had been shut.

'Oh no!' he cried, feeling as if he were rising irresistibly upwards as if coming out of deep water, 'oh, I don't want to wake up!'

He said it out loud, and as he said it he found his eyes were open and he was awake.

15

He lay in a clearing in the heart of the woods. There was nothing in the clearing but high grass, bracken and thistles, all brown and colourless in winter decay. There was a ringing in his ears like the subsiding murmur of a great storm, mixed with calling voices and a far-off tolling like a church bell. Above his head the sky had cleared to a pale, delicate blue.

He knew he had dreamt of events and people of long ago, but as he thought about it and tried to recapture the dream it began to leave him. He had dreamt of the old knight, Robert the Hermit, and the people in the village who must have lived hundreds and hundreds of years ago, but what else?

Peter got to his feet and stretched, picking dried leaves from his clothes and his hair. He was cold. He decided to leave the clearing, which wasn't a particularly pleasant place. He found a rough path through some brambles, passed a notice which said 'Trespassers Will Be Prosecuted', squirmed under some wire, and then fell over something lying half buried in the long grass. It was his bicycle and he was out upon the road. Yes, of course, he had come on his bike, but why?

It was at this point that he remembered the Baxters. He had followed the Baxters: but why had he left the road?

Oh well, it didn't matter greatly, as the Baxters had gone. Of course! They had gone! They had piled their car with boxes and suitcases and he was as certain as he would ever be certain of anything that they would not be coming back again.

He looked down the road – and here for some reason came Janice, also upon her bicycle.

'Oh Peter!' she cried, pedalling up to him. 'Where have you been?'

'Oh, just mucking around,' he answered her vaguely. 'Why are you here? How did you know where to find me.'

'I don't know. I just got a bit worried. Dad said you'd gone out on your bike so I came after you.'

'But how did you know which way I'd gone?'

'I don't know,' she said helplessly.

'How extraordinary,' said Peter, thinking it over. He slowly mounted his bicycle and they pedalled side by side. Pale winter sunlight bathed the country about them in soft, pastel colours.

> 'Something, something climes that lie
> Where day never shuts his eye
> Up in the broad fields of the sky'

sang Peter softly to himself.

'What's that?'

'Poetry.'

'Oh, *poetry*,' said Janice scornfully.

'But it is like that, you see.'

'Whatever do you mean?'

'"The broad fields of the sky" – I almost feel I've been there. Silly, I know. Oh, Janice, I must tell you my dream, if I can remember it. It was something about sleep, white mists coming down and people from long ago, and this old man Robert the Hermit. I'm sure he was once a real person, like Miss Armitage said.'

It was no good. Using words destroyed it more than ever. As he tried so hard to stretch out his hands and grasp it, it dissolved further and further from his vision. Yet he still saw in quite clear detail the figure of the Hermit and his staff and the animals and children surrounding him. To dream about somebody who must have lived so long ago was quite an exciting achievement in itself. It proved he was psychic or something. Perhaps he had fallen asleep over the very place where the Hermit had had his cell once upon a time. And he was feeling amazingly relieved and happy. Of course! He remembered again about the Baxters.

'The Baxters have gone for good,' he said to Janice.

'How do you know? Gone? What do you mean?' she exclaimed sharply.

He told her about the boxes and cases and now he could see himself following the car until it disappeared from view and *knowing* they would not come back. Then he had wandered about here for a time trying to look for a few old stones which might mark where Robert the Hermit had his cell. Miss Armitage would be interested if he did find anything. It was funny that he had had that dream months ago about the old couple in the wood and how like the Baxters they had looked. And now he had dreamt about the Hermit. There was some connection in his mind between the Hermit and the Baxters, but . . . he had the dim sensation of having forgotten something of importance . . . Oh it was annoying the way dreams could be so vivid, stain themselves upon one's sleeping mind and then fade, fade, so that almost nothing was left to cling to . . . Where did one go when one dreamt? What happened?

'What's going to happen to the Baxters' house then?' said Janice. 'They've left all their furniture behind. They can't *really* have gone, just like that can they? I expect they were just making a visit somewhere.'

'They've gone. Gone right away I tell you. Anyway there's not all that much furniture in their house. David and me got in one day when they were out and looked.'

'Peter, you didn't! Whatever would have happened if they'd found you?'

'Well, they didn't, did they?'

They pedalled a few minutes in silence.

'If they really have gone,' Janice burst out at last, 'we needn't move, need we?'

'No. We can stay. We can *stay*, Janice. But I thought you didn't mind the idea of moving anyway.'

'I didn't want to go really. I said it'd be fun to be near the shops and all that, I know, but I didn't want to leave Nut End or the village either. The more I thought about it, the more I didn't.'

'You've got some sense then after all,' he told her, warming to her. Janice was not too bad, he told himself, looking at her with affection. She tried to understand, even if she didn't always succeed. He could have done a good deal worse for a sister. Why, he was quite attached to her in a kind of way, though he could never tell her so. She might get above herself.

'Why thanks,' she said, tossing her head. But she began to hum happily to herself. They whizzed brakeless down a hill and the exhilaration of it made them both break into loud, tuneless song for a few minutes. Then they were faced with a hill which forced them to get off and push their bicycles.

'Why are there people like the Baxters, Pete?' Janice asked in a thoughtful voice, as they struggled up the hill. 'People who just want to be beastly?'

He looked at her and almost said: 'And why are *you* beastly sometimes too?' but knew she would only, and rightly, reply: 'And why are *you?*'

'I don't know,' he replied slowly, gaining time. Her question to him, the oracle, and the trusting look she had given him had indeed rather touched him. It reminded him of the time when she had adored and trusted him in everything: the loving little sister, trotting about to his every command, and hanging on his every word. Those days could never return, and he did not really want them back, but he must not let her down now.

'I don't know why they're beastly, except that they got everything round the wrong way,' he said at last, 'but I do know you shouldn't take too much notice of people like that. It only makes them worse, and you too. It's – it's like the winter. Or a bad wind. It should get better. And if you're lucky it goes away.'

'And they have gone away,' she remarked brightly. 'So it's all right.'

The unspoken question: 'But what if they hadn't?' hovered soundlessly between them for a fleeting moment, then was forgotten and never voiced. Oh, leave the Baxters, bury them deep; tread the earth well in. They had gone; perhaps they had owed money. Perhaps they did not want to pay their creditors. Perhaps, perhaps. They would not return. Smother the unpleasant memory of them. Make the most of one's good fortune.

'Where have they gone, I wonder?' said Janice idly.

'Don't ask no questions and you'll get told no lies,' he sang to her.

'Oh, that's silly. You have to ask questions.'

'But what if the question has no answer?'

She was ahead of him now, standing up to pedal the faster.

'Oh come on,' she shouted back. 'We'll be late for dinner and I'm ever so hungry.'

So Peter came on, and never had home seemed fairer and the prospect of food more appetizing.

'They've gone and left their front door open!' cried Janice as they passed Peacehaven.

Yes, the door of Peacehaven stood gaping and wide, and nobody was within. The red curtain that had bisected the front window had vanished too. The window was blank.

This would be a nine-day wonder in the village but first they must have their dinner.